MAG
AND
OTHER DECEPTIONS

by

Gee Williams

GEE & SON
DENBIGH

© Gee Williams

ISBN 0 7074 0333 2

All rights reserved. No part of this publication may be reproduced, stored in a retrieval system or transmitted in any form or by any means, electronic, mechanical, photocopying, recording or otherwise, without the prior permission of the publisher and copyright holder.

Printed and Published by
GEE & SON,
CHAPEL STREET, DENBIGH

To
DAVID
and in memory of my
MOTHER,
a natural storyteller.

ACKNOWLEDGMENT

Some of these pieces were written for and broadcast by Radio 4. Thanks must go to all at BBC Radio in Cardiff involved in their production but especially to Tanya Nash, whose idea this book was.

Contents

MAGIC	9
SUGAR AND SPICE	14
GYROSCOPE	21
EVERY WORD IN THE BOOK	27
FIREWEED	34
THINKING OF YOU	41
WAITING FOR PERESTROIKA	44
WASTE FLESH	51
'TODAY WE HAVE NAMING OF PARTS'	57
MERCER PREECE (R.A.?) R.I.P.	61
THE MAN MILL	69
SOMEPLACE ON THE VELDT	76
NOM DE PLUME	81
PLASTICITY	88
BALANCE	95
MOTHER DIE	101

YOU ARE HERE

Flintshire is a Brigadoon county – now you see it now you don't. No wonder most people can't place the area on a map. I was born in it but before I left school it had disappeared, been swallowed up by Greater Clwyd. Then, a couple of years ago, out it pops: a little frayed at the edges, it has lost a bit of weight but nothing too unbecoming. Basically it is still a stretched, leanish, strip of land running along one bank of the Dee. From ditch-dredging, boat-building, cattle-rendering Saltney (my home village – only the Dead Sea is further down in the earth's crust) through spit-on-your-hands Shotton and chemical Flint ('so crap they named it twice', A. A. Gill) and on to the peeling painted tarts of Talacre and Prestatyn – the road invites you to keep going, keep your foot down till you hit the 'real' Wales of Celtic gift-shop-assistants, phlegmy sheep-enthusiasts and 'Everything For Your Camping And Climbing Needs' sold to you by a pair of practising crystal-therapists. It must be the only district in Britain whose unofficial capital (Chester) is in another country – and its accent! A phonological nightmare melangé of rural Cymraeg, genteel Cheshire and Scouse.

To be scrupulously honest its copses, fields, hills and valleys are beautiful and in some cases still there – its people no better nor depraved than the rest of humanity. They just happen to be the ones I know.

Magic

"What d'you mean, you get what you pay for?"
"I mean what I say."
"Oh, so this is what I'm worth is it?"
"This is what I can pay for. Even the Co-op wants something now and again. What do I do? Print my own?"

Mam and Dad didn't fight like cat and dog because that's soon over and neither side enjoys it - no, Mam and Dad fought like dog and dog. They were equally matched, they knew each other's moves ... and they only needed to catch breath before they'd be ready for another round and we - Andrew, Mari and me - we had our ringside seats booked every morning we got up.

Just as with dogs, the rows brewed. There'd be a bit of growling over breakfast: the fire not lit, no tea left in the pot, perhaps, but there wasn't much mileage in either of these ... more promising would be how there was only an egg or cornflakes, never any bacon or sausage. Bacon and sausage were better than tea because from bacon and sausage you could move straight on to Money (the lack of, that is). If they could get onto Money before the dishes were in the sink, they were made for the day. By the time Andrew and Mari were ready to take me to the Infants - they'd drop me off on the way to the Big School - Mam and Dad would be at it, shoulders straining, lips drawn back, each one on the look out for that slip, or backward step that would let him or her dart in for a deep, damaging bite.

Oh and no, we never bothered about them hurting each other. Mam was small and terrier sharp, Dad was more bull-mastiff but he'd had an accident up top (he'd been a fitter, not a miner) and hadn't straightened up since before I was born. When we slipped out, often without them noticing, we knew we were leaving behind a fair fight.

Andrew would try to feed his goldfish without being seen (or "Bloody dried ants - cost more than prime steak, pound for pound!" might follow him down the path). Mari and me would call in on Flopsy and load her up with dandelions, putting off for as long as possible the purchase of rabbit food.

Money that was it - the lack of it. They lived on Disability - well we all did - and it was tight and they both wanted to spend. Even when they seemed to be at it over something else like Mrs Morgan always being there in the afternoon, with a steaming cup and a cigarette, it was about Money. In the end Dad would say, "And why can't she stick in 'er own 'ouse and drink 'er own Camp?" which was a kind of coffee essence we had long after everyone else had proper coffee in a tin.

Cigarettes, they were another variation of Money. They both puffed on Woodbines as though they were in a smoking competion which in a way they were. They knew that to give up would mean an easing of the family fortunes, but they could never make up their minds to quit at the same time. After a couple of days Dad would say, "Well if I don't set light to it, she'll only waste it", or Mam would say, "What's sauce for the gander is sauce for the goose," and out would come the Woodies from some secret store.

They argued about us sometimes: "Our Andrew's out of those trousers." "The little 'un wants a new pair of shoes." But we understood we were just proxies. Dad drew his Disability, Mam her family allowance but his was what she needed to keep the house going and she only got it out of him coin by coin.

"Buying so much as a bit of fish, it's a nightmare," I heard her tell Mrs Morgan. "Three and nine, it was - even then there's 'ardly enough for us all to have a sniff of the sea. What 'as 'e given me? Three 'n sixpence. Three and bloody sixpence! I 'ad to ask old Finny Parkin to take an inch off. Could 'ave dropped through the floor, I could."

If breakfast was bad tea (the meal, that is) was a stormcloud that hung over the household all day. We had it at five, presumably because that was when working fathers come home. For Andrew, Mari and me it was a longest hour of the day, that hour between getting in from school and sitting down to eat. It wasn't hunger - we all got free school dinners - it was the thought of the battle lines being drawn up as Mam mashed the swedes still in the cooking liquid or Dad watched her add new lard to the terrible geological layers set in the chip pan.

"And what is this when it's out?" he would enquire softly,

holding a bit of macaroni on his fork as though it was a pupa that might hatch and fly off ... or "I've got turnips, carrots, onions and potatoes here - so who's got my steak and kidney?"

Dad must've learned to cook in the army because at a time when nobody else's father could pour his own glass of beer ours could make an excellent meal, if pushed - liver and onions with the liver so tender that you hardly had to chew it and like a completely different dish to Mam's greasy shoe-leather ... or he could whip up omlettes that were moist and succulent yet with a scalloped, crisp edging thin as a doily's.

More money skirmishes - each meaning to prove a point. Dad's that a good and thrifty housewife could produce splendid meals on next to nothing, and still leave enough for Saturday night at the Miners' Welfare - Mam's that culinary skills were useless without the cash to buy decent ingredients.

Andrew and Mari and me never found out if they were both right or both wrong.

Mam and Dad's hostility rumbled on. It was a subterranean background noise to our childhood, year after year, all year round. But that great festival of stuffing and spending - Christmas - was the time for the semi-molten lava that passed for feelings in our household to burst out and come spewing down the mountainside. We reckoned the days of advent in rituals unknown to the Methodist church. Mid-December Dad might find the presents Mam had sent for out of Mrs Morgan's catalogue ... or a week or so later discover the money he'd passed across week by week had never found its way into Lovage, The Family Butcher's Christmas Club.

"There should be enough there for a capon and a piece of ham," Dad would bellow brandishing the blue book.

"Aye, well you ate that bit of brisket last week knowin' I 'adn't a penny piece. I didn't see you leavin' yours on the side of the plate. Nor that lamb chop."

Mam was clever in her fecklessness. That lamb chop would be sufficient to quell him, because he'd eaten it on a night the rest of us had had an egg each and it had been taken down and used against him and if he carried on he knew Mam would have half a dozen other counts to be taken into consideration.

Christmas dinner, though, was a triumph for Mam in the propaganda wars. It would be two of Mr Morgan's old Rhode

Island Reds bought for a shilling each on Christmas Eve and never stewed for long enough - although to be fair to Mam she'd have probably had to start them in the autumn to make them susceptible to a knife and fork. The meal was, by tradition, eaten in silence. Mam and Dad would not be speaking until well into the New Year, while we children struggled to peel thin grey fibres from whatever bit of hen-anatomy we'd been presented with.

We never wanted seconds and knew better than to complain.

"You can't make a silk purse out of a sow's ear!" Mam would hiss, attacking a chunk of impenetrable breast.

"Oh, is that what it is?" Dad's sigh was directed towards the heavens. "I seem to have got all the bristles then."

The Christmas I was ten something different happened. After we'd all had a go at swallowing the boiled-dry pudding with Mam's special custard that had rhinoceros hide instead of skin, she bundled me into my coat and we went down the road with Andrew and Mari to visit our Gran, Dad's Mam. This we never did unless Mam was desperate to borrow money and all afternoon we sat in the little chilly front room with Mam and Gran eyeing each up while they pretended to take notice of the card tricks Uncle Charlie was showing us. Andrew and Mari also kept exchanging looks over Uncle Charlie's head as they tried to watch Around The World In Eighty Days on Gran's meagre black-and-white.

Uncle Charlie said Dad was the best one in the family at magic and I wondered why he'd never done any for us.

Poor old Gran, who was as careful as her eldest boy, must've been stealing herself to offer us all high tea when Mam announced we were off.

"Of course," she said, "I've nothing in for these children. That son of yours keeps me so short I can barely put bread on the table, never mind a bit of a treat."

"Oh, a good cook can make a meal out of nothing," said Gran which is where Dad must've got it ... but Uncle Charlie went upstairs and came down with all the chocolate he'd brought back from Rotterdam, or somewhere like that - him being in the Navy - and Gran wrapped up half a Madeira cake and some sliced tongue ... and even at ten years old I could understand, now, why we'd been sitting it out at Gran's for hours: it was so Mam could humiliate Dad in front of his brother who wasn't usually home - and by the time Gran told him, Uncle Charlie would be sailing around the Cape Of Good Hope or somewhere else far from Wales thinking about how Dad was starving his own wife and children and there'd be nothing Dad could do.

It was dark and miserable going home but our kitchen welcomed us in, warm and full of delicious smells. On the table Dad had our meal waiting. There was winter salad, which was just cabbage and carrots grated together with a bit of onion, and cold potatoes tossed in oil and vinegar and mustard powder and nutmeg. Best of all there was a huge pie just out of the oven, the crust shiny and brown, the beige gravy bubbling up from a central vent: a savoury well that made our mouths water. Mam sniffed as though she'd just turned vegetarian, but she sat down and set to with the rest of us, kicking her bag and its booty out of sight.

Andrew and Mari chattered on to Dad about the film and how Uncle Charlie had seen a colour television in Hong Kong. But everything Dad said was really meant for Mam's ears (like "Finish that potato - it's a sin to waste food,") while as for Mam, you could see her willing us not to mention chocolate, or suggest a slice of cake. Even when things were going right, they were going wrong in our house. Even when you had a good tea in front of you, it made you feel sick. Before I could be excused I had to mop up the pool of gravy on my plate and show Dad I'd sucked the meat off even the tiniest bones - and there were lots. Mr Morgan must've been breeding chickens with four legs and two sets of wings and these were just the leftovers.

Mam lost interest and let Dad lecture us on the starving millions in the world while she planned the next skirmish, I guess - trying to think up a witty aside about good cooks and hot dinners produced out of thin air.

At last I escaped, and gathered up the cabbage stalks and tough outer leaves and the gravy-soaked bread I'd stowed in my pocket and ran down the wet path to Flopsy.

The hutch was empty.

Sugar and Spice

Exactly where he was or how long he'd been in the water, Ellis couldn't tell. The boat had gone down so quickly. There'd been time to check nothing ... to do nothing. All he knew for certain was that *The Dunlin* had been a couple of miles off Ynys Fach when the explosion ripped her middle out ... and that he (all that remained from The Dunlin above the surface of the Irish Sea) had been swimming and drifting slowly inshore for what seemed like a couple of years ... but he had 'Made it!' He said it aloud.

Made it. That's what mattered. His burned hands now clutched the rock on a level with his head. His numbed feet rested upon a narrow ledge only inches beneath the water. He was not, after all, going to join *The Dunlin* and Mitchell and Pryce.

As he half-lay, half-stood at the base of the cliff Ellis became aware of the waves breaking between his knees ... breaking and pulling at him, although gently. Push... pull, push... pull. There was something so comforting about the rhythm. Push... pull, push ... pull. The rock face sloped inward and he was in no real danger of slipping back. Push... pull, push ... pull, push... pull.

It was some time before it occurred to him that he must have come ashore on the one calm day of the Autumn... this was late September yet here was the sea just slopping about beneath a faint mist. Had he been washed up at this spot the day before, or the day before that, then breakers and coast would've surely combined to smash his body to smithereens.

It was a thought which - together with the swallowed sea water - made him physically and prolongedly sick.

Gradually the murk around and above began to clear. The sun came through to warm both the rocks and the man who clung to them. Ellis felt the sodden shirt release its hold on his back. The general numbness gave way before his body's returning senses. After the tingling there came the pain.

Strangely it was not his hands (which were so obviously injured) but his face which began to hurt soonest.

"Jesus Christ, no!" he cried out, forgetting all relief and gratitude. "Don't let my face be burned!"

Immediately the remembrance of every ravaged face he'd ever seen crowded out all other perception... pilots from World War Two, children on Bonfire Night ... a woman in an old film, scalded with coffee ... that Welsh Guardsman from the Falklands. He cringed against the rock, in greater fear and nearer panic that at any time since he'd gone into the water. He whimpered... and the pain grew.

At last he couldn't bear it. He loosed the rock, reluctantly, with his left hand and brought it down to his face. Gingerly he explored the area of hurt ... it didn't feel burned, although it was rough when he pressed palm against cheek. Pulling away a fragment of what he thought must be blackened skin, he found of all things - a splinter of wood between his fingernails. His face wasn't burned. It was full of splinters.

The pain eased almost at once. Reassured, Ellis was able to relax and it came to him what had happened. The force of the explosion that had driven him backwards from the wheelhouse (and straight overboard) had also implanted particles of The Dunlin's deck in his face - and perhaps in the rest of his body, if he cared to examine it ... only his hands had been caught in the gout of flame. Poor Jacko Mitchell and little Darren Pryce had been - but it was best not to think along those lines.

An unusually large wave breaking across his thighs recalled to Ellis the precariousness of his position. He didn't need to turn around to know that the sea was becoming choppy even as he stood there. If he didn't move, he might still drown, however firm the ledge felt beneath his feet. Finding the strength from God alone knew where, he began to wriggle upwards, hauling with his hands until his stood on tip-toe and had either to slip back or rely upon friction to support him. Without pausing he jerked himself up, found another hand hold and breathed a sigh of relief. With just a slight pressure on his finger tips, the bond between rock and cloth could hold him completely out of the water for the first time in hours. The knowledge put heart into him.

From his new vantage point he realised the climb was going to be easy ... or if not easy, easier than he'd first thought. Only twenty feet or so above his head, the sloping rock wall came to a jagged end. Either there was a ledge up there (offering, at least, sanctuary from the tide) or, more likely on this stretch of coast, there was a strip of raised beach... shingle, probably. If there was a beach he could rest in safety before going on up to look for help. Or someone might find him. Yes - that was it. Someone was sure to find him. With the sun high and the holiday season not quite over, someone would certainly find him.

Perhaps there was someone up there at this very moment ... intent on sunbathing... perhaps all he had to do was shout and they would come ...

Ellis braced himself against the rock and took a deep breath.

The twins had been on the beach since mid-morning. Their mother had been willing to play for a while but when the sun came out she had, as usual, abandoned them and fallen into a trance-like state on her towel. The little girls had understood immediately that there would be no more entertainment from that quarter.

They'd tried to make sandcastles with the stony sand but it was all too dry and wouldn't build. They'd tried to dig a hole with as little success. They'd looked for shells and found none and there was really nothing else they could think of to do. They were sitting close together on a boulder when they heard Ellis's voice - Beth tapping with a pebble, Lucy staring out to sea.

"Help!" he shouted with what remained of his strength. "Help, somebody! Hel-1-p!"

The twins looked first not in the direction the voice was coming from, but at each other. It was an instinctive reaction to whatever occurred, natural as breathing. They laughed softly in secret embarrassment and then looked back at the woman, spread-eagled on the bright cotton. She appeared to be asleep.

They waited a second. She failed to stir.

"Help!" shouted Ellis.

Casually they slipped from the boulder and crept to the edge of the beach on hands and knees.

"Is anybody-?" shouted Ellis and stopped as two identical blonde little heads popped up against the sky. He risked letting go to wave at them excitedly.

"Hello there!" he said in a different tone.

Four grey eyes - grey as the deep water he'd left - gazed down into his.

"You look like angels," he said, smiling although it hurt.

They continued to stare but didn't return his smile.

"Look," he said, "I'm a bit stuck down here, you see. Can you. ..can you go and get someone? Is Mummy or Daddy there? Mm?"

The little pink mouths refused to open and the four grey eyes didn't blink.

"Who's with you, then?" Ellis exhaled in exasperation. "Come on! Don't be shy. Is Daddy with you? Where's Daddy?"

They seemed not to understand the word. My God, he thought, perhaps they're deaf and dumb - or foreigners. Perhaps they can't understand... but, then, they couldn't be there alone, either. Not two children alone in such a place. It wouldn't be safe. Their parents or some other supervising adult must be with them.

"Help!" he shouted more loudly, trying to project the sound above their heads. They flinched in unison and turned anxious glances back up the beach. So there was someone there.

"Help!" Ellis screamed. "Help, somebody! Help! Whoever you are, help!"

When no answer came, he began to claw his way up towards the children, dragging himself on mutilated hands - frustration providing the strength he thought he lacked.

Beth and Lucy watched in fascination as he struggled nearer. Neither dared to speak and yet neither wanted to look away. Beth, the more courageous of the two, was as much interested as afraid... she wondered if the Man-Thing had come out of the sea. There were seals further along the coast that came out of the sea and flopped over the rocks, much as this Man-Thing was doing now.

But the seals were beautiful, of course. Beth liked seals.

Lucy, meanwhile, was feeling only disgust. She watched as the horrible, mangled fingers clutched at the rocks, leaving red prints wherever they touched... and she wished that a big wave would break soon and wash the rocks clean. The eyes that looked up at her were blood-coloured, too. They were small and bloodshot - like pigs eyes - in a scarlet bloated face. And they were getting nearer as the creature heaved itself against the rough slabs - they were getting nearer all the time.

"Help!" Ellis shouted, his voice becoming harsh again as he dismissed the children from his thoughts.

Lucy recoiled as if chastised and Beth, reaching over to take Lucy's hand, let slip the pebble she'd been clutching, allowing it to roll off the edge. Down the rock it clattered, dislodging other loose fragments to fall in a shower on Ellis's upturned face.

"Stop that, you little bitch!" he shouted, trying to blink the grit from his eyes. He was forced to release his handhold to brush at his face and so slipped back a couple of feet before coming to rest, still shaking his head.

Lucy's grasp on her sister slackened also, with relief. More than anything, she wanted the creature to go back down to where it had come from...to stay away from the beach. She shuddered at the thought of its foul red trail across the sand.

She turned to her sister and was rewarded with a smile...and then a broad grin.

As always. No need to say a word.

Beth proceeded to scrape up two small handfuls of sand and this she let pour out slowly onto the Man-Thing's head. It turned away so that most ran down its back instead of into the face, but some stuck on the wispy hair over the forehead. Lucy expected it to shout at Beth but it didn't. Daringly, she sprinkled some sand of her own. When the shower had ceased, it shook itself and began to inch its way across the rocks, away from them.

Lucy tried throwing some more sand but it took no notice. She got to her feet - Beth stood up also - and together they followed its slow progress along the water's edge.

"He won't come up here, will he?" Lucy whispered, nervously. Beth shook her head.

They pushed sand over as they went along and when the sand petered out, small stones - and then larger stones. Most of them missed because the creature kept its face pressed to the cliff and its body also, but a deep red stain appeared at the back of the neck and began to spread across its shoulders. It looked really nasty, Lucy thought. It made her feel sick and she stopped searching for stones and Beth had stopped too.

They waited to see what would happen next.

For a time - it seemed like hours to Ellis - he clung to the cliff and tried to concentrate on hanging on. There was a sharp pain somewhere along his spine and too many other subsiduary pains to locate. Oddly, his face seemed to have stopped hurting.

I must not, he thought, feeling the sting of the waves on the backs of his legs, must not ... must not ... pass out. But his thoughts refused to stay where they were put and into a reconstruction of the last moments in the life of *The Dunlin*, a picture of two small blonde heads would intrude. His boat certainly was lost and he had been in the water and he was injured... but could he really be here, gripping on to the base of ...of some cliff, some...where, being stoned to death by children?

Perhaps, his mind suggested, I've been smashed against the rocks. I ... am... concussed.

As if by way of verification, a trickle of blood ran down the side of his face. His temples began to throb.

I've hit my head, he thought, and I am concussed.

But when he opened his eyes again, four grey eyes looked straight back.

"You little bastards!" he shouted, his self-control deserting him. "I'm going to get up there and wring your bloody necks!"

Instantly the two heads disappeared.

Right, he thought, now I'll do it!

He found new hand holds easily enough. He began to climb.

Lucy squatted on the shingle peering back in the direction from which they'd come. She could still see her mother lying on the coloured towel. The towel was red and black and yellow like the blood and the rocks and the sand. Lucy thought she would never like the towel ... never want it wrapped around her ... never again. She wished she could run straight to her mother, taking Beth with her, of course - but she didn't think she could run on the shingle... not without her shoes. And her legs felt funny... as if they might refuse to run when asked.

Beneath her Lucy could hear the creature as it grunted and puffed.

"It's coming up!" she whispered to Beth - but Beth wasn't there. Beth had retreated from the cliff edge and was some way back, struggling with a ... a thing at her feet. When she moved around to get behind it, Lucy saw that it was a great, oval rock.

It was a beautiful rock - smooth and flattened like a giant plum with pink bits and blue bits embedded in it. Lucy got up on her shaky legs and rushed to help and together the pair of them were able to roll the rock across the shingle. When they reached the edge, Lucy glanced down. Would it see? Would it shout at her again?

Beth watched the Man-thing intently. It was directly under her and much closer now. By edging along it had found an easier place to climb. Soon it would be at the top ... but for the present it seemed concerned with the positioning of hands and feet and wasn't looking up.

Without a sound - without a word - they pushed the rock off.

There was no cry but they could hear the rock go crashing down, bouncing off other rocks before splashing into the sea. Lucy was afraid that it might have missed but when she and Beth peeped over (hands clasped tightly together) an ungainly mass floated face-down in the water. The bundle bumped against the cliff a few times as the sea flopped about. Then a big wave took it under and they ran away because Lucy didn't want to wait and see it come up.

They skipped along the path in front of their mother, chattering and rattling their buckets and spades. A wind had got up and now strong white breakers rushed in from the direction of Ireland. The sun seemed to have lost its warmth.

"There was something in the water," said Lucy suddenly.

"Was there?" her mother asked. "I didn't see anything."

"It was a man," said Beth, "-just a man swimming."

Lucy was shocked. Had it been a man? Just a man, after all? "He wasn't swimming," she said.

Her mother smiled. "And did you speak to him - this man who wasn't swimming?"

"No!" said Beth.

"No? "

They both shook their heads - violently but in perfect unison.

"That's good," said their mother, "because we don't speak to strange men, do we?"

She caught them up, putting a brown hand onto each mop of golden hair.

"My little angels, aren't you?"

It was a phrase the girls always laughed at and, although it reminded Lucy of something not quite nice now, she giggled along with Beth and ran on ahead.

Gyroscope

Carys's friend Kath had been to college - not for very long, of course, because she'd met Sammy and despite his being ten years older and, you'd think, knowing a thing or two, he kept getting her pregnant so Kath was never going to be appearing on University Challenge. But she had been to college and sometimes it showed. It showed, for example, when she said towards the end of the week that the word Giro must have something to do with gyroscope – which was a kind of gadget invented by Leonardo Da Vinci. It had this uncontrollable urge to fly off into space and vanish. This, as Carys always pointed out, was a lot of use when the gas bill had turned red, Daryl and Nicki were agitating for something else the other kids had got – and she didn't even have a couple of quid for fish fingers for Sunday dinner.

"Try tappin' your Ifan," was Kath's school-gate counsel Friday afternoon.

"Don't be bloody daft. Why would 'e 'ave any money? 'E 'ad something off me Wednesday to go down the Club."

"But 'e's 'ad a win since then,' Kath smirked. She didn't even bother with 'I thought you knew' or 'Didn't 'e let on?" She was certain that Carys's boyfriend wouldn't reveal a good win on the ponies, as a matter of course. Her own next-to-useless Sammy would do exactly the same – and that even now he'd got a bit of casual at Mostyn's warehouse.

"'Ow much?"

"'Undred quid, Sammy reckoned. At least. Yesterday - some meeting at ... er ... Chippenham."

"Cheltenham," Carys corrected her, absently.

"Oh well, I don't know – I do the lottery, me. But it was ninety quid, I'm telling you."

"Can't be - where's the stake gonna come from for a win like that? And I thought you said it was a hundred?"

"Ninety, a hundred – what's the difference? And you gave it

'im Wednesday. Lager money ... only it wasn't. Any road he put it on an... accumulator. You put a bit on the first and then-"

"I know 'ow the soddin' things work," Carys shouted. I know all that. Yankies, doubles, I know every soddin' one!"

Both of them glanced around guiltily to see if a teacher was in earshot but there was still no sign of them or the school's inmates. No-one even looked over from amongst the assembled mothers and toddlers. Only a new-born baby, surely no more than three or four weeks old, seemed to react, screaming genteel shock into the cold air. A quick shuffling inside its mother's stained coat and it subsided, mouth full.

"Christ, she's not feedin' it 'ere, is she?" Kath said, as much to change the subject as anything.

"Oh, it's that dirty piece - Denise something. Do anything anywhere, that's 'er. Let's 'ope poor Derek don't come out now or 'e'll be getting a free biology lesson."

Derek Rogers was the headmaster, a slight, softly-spoken man whom the mothers all had down as a bit of an innocent, easily shockable, that sort of thing. That his working life involved a daily interface with domestic violence, incest, theft, bullying and glue-sniffing - particularly glue-sniffing which was now sweeping through The Emlyn Williams County Primary School as an outbreak of measles would have done in years gone by - never occurred to any of them.

"Ninety quid, you say?"

"Oh, at least," Kath affirmed with satisfaction.

"So where the bloody 'ell is it?"

"Got it on 'im, I expect. That's what mine does."

"Na - 'e's down at The Wanderers, trainin'. It'd get nicked if 'e took it there. There's no locks on them lockers."

"Stashed then".

"Oh, right. That's a big 'elp. It's stashed, but where the 'ell is it? Where's the tight bugger stashed it? That's what I want to know. It'd make all the difference just now, ninety quid."

"Oh get 'er!" Kath laughed. "When wouldn't it?"

Carys's cheeks burned so that the freckles were momentarily lost on her white skin. Her eyes focused on some unseen other.

"Right, well, you bastard. Two can play at that game," she muttered.

Without further comment she dived into the oncoming tide of

children that had been released by the opening of some floodgate deep within the cavern of the building. She extracted two red-haired, sulky, short creatures by the arms and delivered them up to Kath like captives. "Drop these off at me mam's will you? Tell 'er I'll be along later to pick 'em up. Tell 'er she could give 'em their tea. Tell 'er .... Tell 'er I'm a bit short and I've nothing in they like."

There was nothing 'in' at home which made it that much easier emptying both of the kitchen cabinets. Not that there was any point, because Ifan wasn't going to leave money any place that she looked... but then maybe he'd been clever... thinking that's what she'd think...

She piled back the three pans, chipped unmatched dishes and the broken toaster still rattling with its full complement of fossilised crusts, letting them topple onto and squash a new box of tea bags and a packet of dried milk. The big jar of coffee, though, was rescued from the dishes-slide and emptied out onto the worktop. She didn't drink the stuff and Ifan did - but there was only a pungent, brown powder under her hands as she scooped most of it up.

The fridge was easy. Two sweaty rashers of bacon entombed in plastic lay beside a tub of cheap margarine. In the door was a mainly-used jar of maroon jam and a bottle of chocolate milk.

In the ice-box there was ice.

She'd seen a film once about a man who'd hidden diamonds in a freezer... great big diamonds nestling amongst all those things that rich people and criminals have in their freezers... whole young animals and giant cakes and salmon the size of sharks... This is stupid, she thought. Of course he'll hide it in his own stuff. But she pulled out the fridge anyway, just to check that its fluffy pipes and workings lay undisturbed.

Upstairs it was surprising how little Ifan's own stuff amounted to. She'd never noticed before how she and the kids seemed to occupy the whole house. In the bathroom, for instance, all the scented soaps and foams and oils her mam bought her for Christmas and her congealed pots of make-up filled most of the shelf - that and the kids' no-sting shampoo and Nicki's giant sponge duck and Daryl's water-pistol.

On the windowsill there was just an old Gillette razor and a bar of soap with dark stubble dried in it.

No one in their right mind would hide anything in the kids' room, even if they could get inside. There were two single beds with two wooden boxes that, in theory, contained their toys and games. They didn't need wardrobes because both of them went through clothes so quickly, they were either being worn, being washed, or airing on radiators, ready to put on next day.

The big bedroom she shared with Ifan seemed the obvious sanctuary for immigrant cash. Her fingers flew through the contents of drawers fingering and discarding underwear, jumpers, teashirts and tights. Why start on her own clothes? She caught her reflection in the mirror, flustered yet intent. Because she was saving it up. Saving up that moment when her hands would curl around the hard cylinder of notes - when she'd find his stash (oh let it be in fives and tens) and slide it into the tight pocket of her jeans ... and then she'd walk around with it, just around the house for a while, letting it dig into her buttock every time she moved or tried to sit ... and then she'd saunter over to her mam's, conscious of it all the time, and pick up the kids and buy those pizzas they liked on the way back even if they'd had their tea. She wouldn't be able to treat her mam, though she'd like to, because she'd borrowed off her again this week and she might want paying back.

And it wouldn't be stealing. How could it be stealing? That money belonged to her, by right.

Now Ifan's side. His old 501s, that he had before they met, were clean and folded in one drawer, their pockets empty. Three rolled-up socks each held only another sock within. Jockeyshorts, including the pair which said WARNING! STICK OF DYNAMITE in spiky letters, contained nothing of interest. His Wanderers striped number nine shirt - which he'd want clean for tomorrow afternoon - lay caked in mud under the bed with his Nikes. The two black sweatshirts she'd got down the market and which he wore only when there was nothing else, hung in the wardrobe with his old leather jacket.

There were no winnings. Not anywhere.

In fury she pulled the pillows from their cases, the quilt from its cover, the mattress from the bed, sending up a cloud of dust that had her sniffing and sneezing, panting with effort.

The lounge - that's where it must be - where they all lived and ate and watched television and argued and had the occasional laugh. Or at least she and the kids did. There weren't many evenings you'd find Ifan in there, not after he'd fed his face. Funny how it had only just struck her - that when she thought of their being all together, home, under the same roof, how Ifan was not in the picture. How that razor and the few bits of clothing made it seem as though she had an overnight guest, someone just crashing down between here and there. She'd never stayed in a hotel but she bet people took more stuff on holiday than Ifan had in his own house.

There was nothing of his downstairs, nothing of his down the sides of the two sofas that clashed, nothing under the T.V., nothing stuffed behind the stereo, nothing taped to the back of the picture of the kitten playing with the bright butterfly on the impossibly green lawn. She laid out the felt-tipped pens, the key to God-knows where, the coins and Nicki's hair slides that were her trove on yesterday's paper. That was his, of course, or had been. Today's would be out with him - handy for checking the form.

In desperation, she crawled on hands and knees around the room, tugging at the carpet which seemed securely fixed, scanning the underside of the ugly old dining table and chairs, finally lying flat on her back to stare up at the plastic light fitting ...

Huge, unwanted tears formed, overflowed and took the shortest route down, trickling into her ears. The money was nowhere. Gone - either poured down the gullets of Ifan and the rest of his so-called mates in The Wanderers ... or back in some bookie's safe, recycled on a sure thing in today's two-thirty. It had been just another case of Kath's famous gyroscope - a thing with this uncontrollable urge to fly off into space, to vanish.

"Christ Almighty Carys! What you doin' down there, girl?"

Ifan's voice came so loudly, so unexpectedly, it seemed to fill the room. Carys tried to jump to her feet and banged her head.

"What's the matter? You come over sick or something?"

"What? No - Don't be so bloody daft. Course I'm not sick. No bloody time to be sick, 'ave I? And don't panic - I'm not 'aving another. Anyway ... I've gotta go and pick up those two we got , 'aven't I? 'Ad to palm 'em off on their gran, 'ope she'd give 'em their tea 'cos I couldn't. And, you're back early. Done yourself an injury 'ave you? There's bugger all in the 'ouse anyway. You'll 'ave to make yourself a bacon butty till I get potatoes off Mam."

"No need," Ifan said and grinned.

"Oh full on the drink, is it? Nice for some. Well, I'm off to get the kids."

"No need," he said again.

"Oh, well, they're-"

"I've seen your mam. She'll keep 'em tonight. I took round fish and chips. Took 'er a nice bit of scampi and a bottle. That sweetened 'er up."

"You! Bought their tea?"

"All right, I know. Once in a blue moon. But don't go gettin' stroppy - I've 'ad a bit of luck. See?"

Casually he strolled over to the gas fire which was always off these days because they were so far behind with the bills. In the gap where the wooden surround met the old tiles of the grate, a buff envelope had been posted. Ifan tweaked it out.

"I was keeping this till tomorrow - proper night out, Saturday and all that, then I thought, Sod it! That big sweeper they got playing for Athletic'll probably cripple me in the first 'alf - he's a brickie or something, looks like Rambo. So let's do it tonight, Ifan, I thought. There's over a hundred and twenty quid 'ere girl. I've 'ad a win. Get tarted up and that's you and me out on the town. Oh, no 'ang on." He rummaged in the envelope, his big, blunt fingers unaccustomed to telling notes. "That's thirty quid for Mr Gasman and the rest for us."

"You know," he said, patting Carys's bottom as she trotted ahead of him, still speechless, up the stairs. "You must be slipping love. I'd've laid odds on you finding this before now."

Every Word in the Book

"Snow – this is the thing, Mrs Jone."

Mr Al Ghamdi was the best non-native speaker of English I'd ever encountered but he never could get that final s.

"I'm sorry Mr Al Ghamdi?"

"Already it is January tenth. I am without snow."

Mr Al Ghamdi gestured towards the window by way of explanation: bare oakwoods bordered our college campus. A bitingly cold wind straight off the Irish Sea was punishing the higher branches but I had to admit there was no evidence of the frozen object of desire lying about in picturesque heaps.

"You said snow . . . in the winter. Last September when we did the story of Mr London."

"Jack London, yes. To Light a Fire – the man and the husky . . . Mm. But I did say, if you remember, that it was set in Northern Canada –"

"And you said that there would be snow," he persisted.

"Did I?"

"And you gave us this card." Patiently Mr Al Ghamdi removed from his briefcase a Christmas card, still in its slit envelope and handed it across the desk. With reckless self-incrimination I had written: 'To the Higher National Diploma English Group.' Inside I knew what I would find – a photograph of Cadair Idris metres deep in the white stuff with Season's Greetings emblazed across the top . . . and my signature. At the time it had seemed smartly sensitive for a class of Saudi Arabians.

"I have bought," he said, paused and then corrected himself, "I have since bought skis, ski-sticks, ski-boots, ski-hats, ski-eye-protection and ski-suits for myself and Samira," Samira I had met – she was Mr Al Ghamdi's beautiful wife, "and for Nadir and Mohammed all of these things and also a –" there was a further pause while Mr Al Ghamdi consulted that truly vast store of words that was his English vocabulary, "a sleigh or sledge."

"But . . . but – that must've cost a fortune. I mean an absolute bomb!"

Got him! Mr Al Ghamdi may well have had a mental dictionary that rivalled Shakespeare's but this idiomatic 'bomb' caused his eyes to widen in alarm.

"Bomb?"

"It's slang. It means a lot of money."

I watched him file it away. Tonight – I knew – he would be saying to his twin boys, "Do not fight with your ski-sticks, Nadir and Mohammed. They cost a bomb." To me he said, "It is unimportant, the expense. But in June we will all return home. I must have snow."

"Yes . . . yes. Of course you must," I said, glancing away. My open book offered no comfort. Twentieth Century Short Stories with its piece by good old Jack-bury-me-out-on-the-tundra-London was what had got me into this fix in the first place. Around the door the next batch of students – an arts course by the look of their frightening gear – had assembled to take possession of the room. "O.K. Right. Well, the thing is, Mr Al Ghamdi . . . the thing is that here, on the Wirral Peninsula, the climate is quite mild."

Mr Al Ghamdi appeared dubious. I didn't blame him. For the last two winters, since the college had begun its economy-drive, the temperature inside the lecture halls could only be described as chilly. I pressed on. "This means that we may not get snow in these parts . . . certainly not enough to ski or sledge. You'd have to drive a good way . . . say the Lake District or . . . or your best bet would be over the border into Wales. Not that there'd be a problem!" I added quickly, remembering the previous autumn when the whole group requested help in obtaining visas to see Blackpool Illuminations.

"Thank-you. But I do not speak the language."

"That's O.K. Neither do I and I was born there."

"Ah, yes, Jone," he mused, "You told us this was the commonest Welsh name although there is no jay in the Welsh language . . . and you cannot speak it anyway . . . I see. You will tell me where and when to go?"

I bit back the casual reference to the weather-forecast, partly out of guilt. I mean Saudi students were well-provided for by their companies, but how much had the poor man spent? And there was something else: the knowledge that had our positions been reversed and I'd a yearning to visit an oasis or just see the stars from the desert at night, Mr Al Ghamdi would have had Mrs Jone and Mr Jone – and any other members of the Jone family that cared to tag along – savouring the experience within twenty-four hours.

"O.K. Fine. Let me get in touch with a friend of mine." The friend was Lynne Lockley who had given up the academic rodent race years ago and now ran a climbing school in Snowdonia with her husband, an escaped geology don. "I'll ring Lynne and Siôn," I told Mr Al Ghamdi. "There's a ski-slope just down the valley from them. First whiff of snow and they'll let me know."

Mr Al Ghamdi smiled politely at the whiff usage with such an un-pungent object. "Thank-you. You are most kind. But – but if we are not in residence, how will you leave a message? The snow may melt."

Mr Al Ghamdi's employer's had rented a house for the family not far from the college and he could often be seen scuttling home between lectures to sort out the latest domestic emergency. Samira, I guessed, was used to staff.

"I'll put a message through the door – through the letter box."

"The same thing, I think," he said.

Of course that January and February proved the warmest on record. We at the college needed no Met Office minion to verify the evidence of our senses. On many a bright afternoon, students from all over the Middle East could be seen crossing the campus minus their overcoats – while the native contingent were down to an Oxfam sweatshirt or jumper and jeans. Mr Al Ghamdi – ever courteous – made no further reference to sledging and skiing. But I imagined I caught a reproachful look when I mentioned the weather. Jack London had been returned to the dust of the stockroom and replaced by English Passages for Science Students – paralysingly dull but mercifully free of any snowy allusion. The sun shone. The Easter vacation beckoned. All I had to do, I thought, was to drag the class through another couple of "Irrigation: boon or bane?" type essays and spring would have truly arrived to heal all hurts. Not even Mr Al Ghamdi could yearn for the big freeze with the daffodils doing the rumba and the light playing on the two great estuaries that almost made an island of The Wirral – the Mersey and the Dee.

And then it happened: the first Thursday in March the phone was ringing as I entered our cottage. "It's Siôn," said an unfamiliar voice. "Lynne's gone into Caernarfon to stock up. There's just a dusting on the tops but more on the way."

"A what?" I asked, pretty stupidly. "There's a what on the where?"

"A dusting of snow . . . on the tops of the hills," he said extra-slowly. "It's for skiing on – for someone you know – which is why I am calling. Prynhawn da."

"Oh, good afternoon to you too. Even I know that one," but Siôn had gone.

Not for the first time I thanked my guardian angel that I was not Lynne, that I was not having to go down into Caernarfon to stock up and that I was not running a climbing school in my native country and married to Siôn Lockley. Then I dialed Mr Al Ghamdi and gave him the glad news.

"Is snow there now?" he asked.

I couldn't blame him for his scepticism. It was five o'clock with a clear, petrol-blue sky overhead. "Very well, we will set out at once."

"Oh no, leave it till tomorrow. Your children'll be dead on their feet."

"I'm sorry?"

"You're children will be too tired."

"Then they will sleep."

"Well you have the map. Remember – The Pennant Climbing School. Ask for Lynne Lockley and please give her my regards . . . and don't forget to ask for a family room."

"What other rooms are there?"

I felt unequal to explaining the delights of bunk-house accomodation to Mr Al Ghamdi but the prospect of six beery students from Manchester joining the little Arab family at midnight made me stress the point.

"Other rooms are less good. A family room. Tell Lynne."

"I will recollect the term. Thank-you for your trouble."

"No trouble," I said. "Good luck."

By morning The Wirral was white. Not just tastefully

sprinkled with white, so that every raw modern house became a pretty rural retreat and every garage a woodcutter's hut. No, rather it was blanketed in a deep, crushing weight of white that blocked even the major roads and collapsed inwards from each opened door. Trains were cancelled. Buses failed to appear. All the schools declared a holiday and, much to my relief, the college closed too.

Mr Jone and I celebrated with a second course of breakfast, watching on television (with unconcealed shadenfreude) the chaotic scenes from Northern England and North Wales . . . North Wales!

Mr Al Ghamdi.

Poor Mr Al Ghamdi . . . last heard of, like Scott of the Antarctic, setting off for the icy unknown. I ran to make the call, even as the superior London voice intoned "power and telephone lines down throughout the region . . ."

The Pennant Climbing School responded with a continuous tone and some static.

Later in the day, even the tone disappeared.

People always say at such times, "I imagined the worst," but the actual details of the worst as it had befallen the Al Ghamdis no one could've come up with.

It began – like all good horror stories – with a missed turning. Somewhere beyond the little town of Capel Curig and only ten miles from his destination, Mr Al Ghamdi had lost his way. "Certainly the road became less good," he conceded – five days later, " but I believed that by continuation I would surely find the left turn that I must make."

This of course is far from a winning strategy in Wales where many roads simply go up into the mountains and stop when they can get no further . . . rather like Mr Al Ghamdi, in fact. But the least I owed him was to listen to his story and not interrupt with I-could've-told-you-that . . . if only because I hadn't when it might have done some good.

"The snow was falling in much larger pieces by now," he said "and it was quite dark . . . and then, in the distance, we saw a light and I said, 'Look, there is the friend of Mrs Jone'."

"But it wasn't?" I knew it wasn't. Lynne had not set eyes on them . . . which is why I'd had the police and R.A.F. scouring Snowdonia for their blue estate car – in between rushing pregnant women to hospital and feeding thousands of starving sheep.

"Then where have you been?"

"It was a place called Fferm Argoed Bach," he said with perfect pronounciation. "It means 'the small farm within the enclosure of the trees' although there did not appear to be trees around it. It was a small farm. A low house – inside, you understand?"

"A cottage?"

"Yes, a cottage . . . and there was also a long ysgubor."

"Ysgubor?"

"Yes, an ysgubor. A stone ysgubor . . . with hay and many sheep and their lambs."

"A barn? You've spent five days in a barn?"

"Oh, no. We have been in the cottage – the bwthyn or tŷ bach. We have stayed with the family."

"Oh, thank-goodness! So you stopped at this place, and they took you in and you've been there until . . .?"

"This morning. A machine polished the road and we drove back. It required some solicitude." He looked modest. "I came to college because I knew that you would be concerned."

"Mr Al Ghamdi, you shouldn't have. Go home and rest. Is your family all right?"

Mr Al Ghamdi smiled, always ready to discuss them.

"Oh quite well – that is extremely well. The boys and my wife were made comfortable . . . the old lady in the house, I think, liked children very much."

"You were with an elderly couple?"

"A man and his mother. She is ninety-two years old."

"Good grief. How old was the son?"

"This he did not tell us, but old, I would say. Much older than my father. But strong. Each day I went with him to feed his flock in the ysgubor and he could raise many, many more packages of hay than myself.

"Bales," I said,

"Sypynnau?" asked Mr Al Ghamdi. When I looked blank he continued, "that was the word, I think. It was not always easy because his English was suffering from disuse. His mother spoke none at all."

"Oh no! You poor things! You must've been going mad, stuck

up there all this time. I'm so sorry. I really am. I felt so bad for sending you, and then when you were lost . . . and well . . . now you tell me it turned into The Rocky Horror Show and–"

Mr Al Ghamdi shook his head. "But this is not true! Everything has been quite excellent. Mr Trefor and Mrs Trefor have been of outstanding kindliness. They had smoked muttons, and sacks of rice and potatoes and onions and beans and my wife and Mrs Trefor made food that we eat at home. I and the boys helped with the agriculture."

"But what did you do? You must've been bored out of your minds."

"But we all learned Welsh!" said Mr Al Ghamdi. "The boys are very quick and can speak without thought, whereas I am in the stern of their aptitude. But as soon as I learned 'Beth ydy?' – what is? – 'yn Gymraeg' – in Welsh – my progress became speedy. In addition to knowing five hundred nouns with their genders I can say 'Ddim diolch' – no thank you – 'Dych chi'n hoffi?' – do you like? – 'Mae'r plant yn hoffi' – my children like. Oh, Mrs Jone, it is a beautiful language! 'Mae hi'n oer heddiw' – it is cold today. 'Roedd hi'n oer ddoe' – it was cold yesterday. 'Ble dych chi'n byw?' – where do you live . . . ?"

And on he went. On and on and on.

Fireweed

When she'd placed the washed mug upside-down on the draining board and laid the spoon along the runnel in the stainless steel parallel to the knife and swept the orange peel into the bin, she allowed herself to slump into the window-seat. This must be the six or seventh day in a row she'd forced herself to eat breakfast... (as Dr Parry said: small victories, that's what she must concentrate on. Forget the bigger picture).

But outside - across the lane - they were busy touching up the bigger picture and it was a landscape not to her liking. Today, Willa noted, they were taking off the last of that most spectacular of wild flowers, Chamaenerion augustifolim - the fireweed.

There was no use objecting - she'd found that out a year ago.

What, after all, was she going on about? A forgotten half-acre of ground... with its bird-sown shrubs and its wind-sown weeds. Was that all? Who cared about that wilderness?

Well she did...

She *did*.

The fireweed was being thrown into a dazzling mass of purple blooms that for a day or two would grace the heaps of builder's rubble. One of the men stopped and straightened up. He eased his back in that age-old attitude workmen have adopted since before they laid out the garden round the Sphinx. It wasn't his fault, of course, and yet Willa couldn't help wishing something hurtful and chronic upon his spine, like a slipped disc... or a trapped nerve – even better. A pain without a pathology. From the body to the brain.

Just as her own nails stabbed at her innocent palms...all the while...were stabbing now...

There were laws to stop this - but these seemed stacked against anyone trying to save anything - and what had she tried to save but an absence, a vacancy? And there was public opinion, which in this case meant local people - her neighbours - whose disinterest lay on the village like a musty old blanket. In fact, if they had any feelings at all, they were on the opposite side. The two next door were prime examples of that: Mary and Elwyn - Nosy and Uncaring.

"Not at work, today, eh?"

This after Willa'd been at home for her sixth month and it was becoming obvious to herself and the company that she wouldn't be returning. ("Look for something less demanding" was Dr Parry's advice). Mary was always on watch, always ready to pop out of the too-close back door: "Your milk's still on the step!" "Lettin' your hair grow are you?" and "Have you lost weight?" Mary had this terrible knack for high-lighting self-neglect - that continual temptation since release from hospital. Even placing the uneaten meal on the bird table became something to do after dark.

"Lovely bungalow, they're putting up," Elwyn would nod across the road at the foundations which in early spring could've passed for an archaeological dig. "Double garage, by the looks of it."

"Very fitting."

"What? Oh, yes! Well that's what it used to be, didn't it? When Mary and me came here after the war it was Tudor's Garage - petrol pumps, the lot. You wouldn't remember?"

"No, it'd been flattened - greened over. Fireweed, that's what I remember. A huge sweep of it. That's why I bought the-"

"Oh, yes. A right mess it's been all these years. Nice to see it cleared up."

'Cleared up' was one way to describe what had been done to the neglected plot. 'Developed' was how most of the official answers to her letters defined it. 'There could be no planning objection to the development of a site that had formerly been Tudor's Garage...and before that Coed Coch Cottage.' She'd discovered this herself at the County Archive after two bus journeys that had left her trembling and terrified.

It was years since she'd travelled by bus ... a fat woman with a big orange holdall had sat next to her, trapping her, letting the bag touch her arm as the vehicle jolted and swerved for no reason. That bag had become a torment, tap, tap, tapping against her elbow until it began to sting and then to burn - really to burn as though it were as hot as its colour. She had cowered against the cold metal of the bus, but the woman's bulk simply

spread in relief at the added space so that Willa had had to jump up, breathless, hardly able to get out the jumbled mixture of apologies and lies about missing the stop.
("Driving? Out of the question? Not with what you're on!"
"No, doctor. I suppose not.")
. . . If only she'd been mobile - able to confront these green belt officers and conservation officers and tree preservation officers in person - perhaps their failure to preserve or conserve anything green might have been brought home to them. Someone could have done it. She could have done it herself before the ... well. (Dr Parry always called it 'this illness.') But no one had done it and now, to the cement mixer's back-beat, a lorry with a giant grab was unloading pink and grey flagstones and stacking them in separate piles where this time last year, the buddleia bushes had bloomed.
"Nice mornin'."
The driver's greeting sent her ducking back into her own doorway, almost trapping finger ends in confusion and haste. The tiny panes in her front window with its rippled eighteenth-century glass provided a better vantagepoint. From here she could watch safe from the man's frank, appraising eyes: the glass-blower's blemishes flicking across the unwelcome activity as she moved her head.
The bungalow must be nearing completion. Today the entire workforce of 'Watkin and Sons, General Builders' were paving the area in front of that double garage so much admired by Elwyn. It would soon resemble a giant chessboard. The garage itself was as big as her own cottage.
Willa smiled nastily. If she could still bear to walk about, talking to people, she could engage the new owners in polite conversation and suggest they give the garage a singular name. Clutch Cottage or Sparkplug Place. "After all," she imagined herself saying in a friendly tone, "the thing's so huge it'll probably be allocated its own postcode."
Already she hated the bungalow's owners. She had resigned herself to another pensioner duo, gardening and gossiping quietly all week and invaded by hoards of grandchildren, dumped for weekends. But the blonde in the bright yellow American jeep landed in the lane like some exotic bird blown off course. Her skirt was so short beneath the blue of the tailored

jacket Willa thought at first she must've forgotten to put it on - the effect was that of a Principal Boy in an old-fashioned pantomime.

Mary, of course, had all the details terriered out before the drains were laid: husband in the clothing business, away a lot, wife a former-model. "What for?" Willa had snapped, "Barbie-dolls?" but Mary hadn't heard or hadn't understood and pressed on, "Lovely girl. No side to her at all - plenty of money about, but natural as they come. Runner-up to Miss Chester, nineteen-eighty-nine. Gail-Ann Bragg as she was then."

When Mr Runner-up Miss Chester put in an appearance he was a weasel-faced little man, a good twenty years older and looked to Willa's eyes like nothing so much as a failed Tory Euro-M.P.

Mid-morning a kitchen-fitters' truck arrived. The flagstone lorry met it in the lane, grinding up what remained of the grass as the pair of juggernauts edged past, brushing flanks as though about to mate. Over coffee in the window seat Willa was able to enjoy a low-level skirmish as the huge, flat boxes that the units came in drifted onto the raw earth waiting to be paved. Watkins' small army kicked and shoved them back only to have them returned in greater numbers by the wind.

By six the site was quiet ... the heap of wilted fireweed testament to the day's work. A thrush sang in Elwyn's apple-tree until startled into silence by the carnivorous flap of a piece of cardboard at Willa's gate. The lane seemed deserted and she risked a daylight foray to tidy it away.

There were boxes and pieces of box everywhere - lying on the grass verge, flipped up against the hedge, flopping and tumbling across the pink-and-grey drive. Why should she be responsible for them? ... and yet with this strong north-westerly freshening as it cooled, the cardboard would be distributed throughout the village by morning ...

She'd come back - that was it. She'd wait for dusk when nothing she did could be observed or cause comment. There'd be no Elwyn or Mary sidling out especially to call, "Oh, havin' are tidy up are we?" No leering spotty youth from the tied-cottages to murmur "Watcha" whilst avoiding eye-contact. No Pat and Steve from the Post Office to shout "Hello stranger, where you bin hidin'?" No couple from the stables-conversion looking her up and down, wondering if she was the sort that might feed their cat or water their plants.

She'd come back.

When darkness fell she stubbed out her cigarette and emptied the ash-tray into the pedal bin, so that the squashed filter-tips and spent matches rained down onto the still-fragrant curls of orange peel. There was nothing else. That tin of soup she really had meant to eat sat unopened on the worktop... It was too late to bother, even if her stomach had not been telling her No need! No need!

Upstairs she lit the lamp in her bedroom and turned all the others off. Now the little cottage looked innocent and unassailable. Willa Thomas, who everyone knew to be a bit strange since her illness, had taken herself off for an early night. Within minutes she was through the back gate and into the fields.

She was used to being out at such times. For the last few months she'd taken to walking the fields and woods around the village even when to those snugly settled in front of their T.V.'s the night appeared pitch black... because it never was. Once your eyes became used to the gloom it was never pitch black - the trees and hedgerows stood out from one another in deepening shades of charcoal against a sky that could be splattered with stars or palely clouded - or that strange no-colour - the colour of closed eyelids - moonless, overcast and yet still touched by the faint glow of a distant universe. As for underfoot, well, you had to remember the path... and hope nothing had fallen across it since your last jaunt.

The field she was crossing had just given up its hay-crop and the sweet smell of the dying grasses was everywhere on the wind - then she was over the gate into sheep pasture - even easier walking above a sharp scent of old feta-cheese and lanolin. Through two wire fences and she was in the lane, directly opposite the footpath that skirted Aaron Wynn's full Dutch barn - and led to the bungalow's rear. She had walked for nearly a mile and was now across from her own home ... but unseen, unguessed at and with a heart pounding at the small effort.

She'd not come here to do what she did now. Perhaps it was the sudden familiar rattle of the cigarettes and matches in her coat pocket ... or the seductive way torn bits of cardboard skittered about her ankles ... and then there was the noise: the rattling of each individual sheet of corrugated iron that roofed Aaron's hay... the Cola cans barrelling out from the bus-shelter and the roar of that north-westerly, coming straight off the Atlantic and hitting the tops of the poplar trees.

The breaking window hardly registered at all.

She hadn't slept, of course, but had changed into sensible striped pyjamas, knowing she'd be called out.

"Willa! Quick!" someone called and another pebble bounced off the window-pane.

She ruffled her own hair before pushing up the sash.

"The bungalow!" Mary shrieked unnecessarily. "The bungalow's on fire!" Mary made a comic figure - a fat little pink parcel of candlewick, capering around Willa's front garden, her rollers in constant motion.

"Elwyn got up to ... you know - with his prostate - and he came back shouting 'The bungalow's on fire!'"

Elwyn and his prostate were loitering as near as they dare to the beloved double garage. The bungalow certainly was on fire. Huge, ragged tongues of flame darted out from several windows. There was a Bonfire Night noise of wood crackling and a marvellous Bonfire Night smell. Even as Willa watched, the roof of the jutting wing she knew to be the kitchen heaved a sigh and collapsed. She and Mary gazed transfixed as a plume of glowing embers shot skywards, were received by the wind and laid neatly down the lane onto Aaron Wynn's giant Swiss roles of winter fodder.

"Call the fire brigade!" Mary shouted.

"Oh, yes, I will. Just a minute. Tell Elwyn to keep back. I'll come down."

It was really bad luck on the Runner-up to Miss Chester, nineteen-eighty-nine, thought Willa. Her dream home catches light and the first people to notice haven't got a phone.

"It's the empty house across the road," Willa told the operator, "it's burning down."

"And where are you?"

Dutifully she revealed - enunciating with slow precision - her name, address and number.

"And the property on fire?"

"Well I don't really know - it hasn't got a name ... not finished you see." She hoped the fire brigade kept a sort of sliding scale for emergencies and that this one wouldn't rate too highly. "Just come into the lane from the main road - I think they'll be able to tell which it is."

She pulled on her trench coat but kept the slippers as a touch of authenticity. She joined Mary outside.

"You were a long time. Are they on their way?"

"Of course. They kept asking me questions."

"I mean a long time comin' to the window."

"Sleeping pill, I'm afraid. Leaves you dead to the world."

Dead to the world, that's what she'd wanted to be. That's why when she crossed her hands inside her sleeves as though chilled by the breeze, her fingers found ugly raised scars on both wrists. But tonight they didn't pull and ... yes, they seemed that bit softer as she probed them, healing from within as Dr Parry had promised they would.

By the time the engine arrived most of the village was assembled - Pat and Steve from the Post Office, saying "Hello stranger," as they joined her - the spotty kid from the tied-cottages, trying to get a look inside her trench coat, and the Caddock family from next door who'd brought a dog on a rope and a small child in a push-chair. The couple from the stables-conversion were actually talking to Elwyn about doing a bit of gardening for them. Aaron Wynn came down with his two sons in the Landrover, just in time to see them give up on the bungalow and then fail to save his hay.

Some of them she'd not spoken to for nearly a year but now ... well it was funny, really ... now she found she had a nod and a "Terrible isn't it?" for each of them... and all the time she was out there with the heat on her face and the smoke tickling the tiniest passages of her lungs and being coughed up in dry, cheek-reddening spasms, all that time she was feeling so... hungry.

Thinking of You

Evan and Marcy have been so kind - made all the arrangements - dealt with the paperwork - and even put on this spread that Marcy and her mother (who must be in her sixties) are now clearing away.

There go the egg sandwiches, just starting to curl. Evan, helpful even in distraction, is retrieving the fruitcake, mouthed and deserted on the mantel-shelf as he chats to his mother-in-law.

They're just cousins, after all, and Marcy only by marriage. But they were on the spot - that was the thing - and what with Evan being a chef and Marcy working for social services, well they have the skills, don't they? You couldn't imagine a couple better equipped to organize a funeral. In fact, they're so well-qualified they might go into business...'The Complete Funeral Company - everything attended to from that first unpleasant task of discovering the body to that last little detail of obscure dietary requirements amongst the mourners.

Aged aunties with imaginary egg-allergies and sulky Vegan teenagers a speciality. Let us deal smoothly and discreetly with your Uncle Emlyn when he wonders aloud what the oak dresser might fetch! Let us spirit away every last bottle of sherry just at the point a party-atmosphere breaks out ... Let us-'

I think I'm getting hysterical.

It'll be the Prozac and the Temazipam last night (after what I found, I needed it) and then there were the two large gin-and-tonics on the way to The Crematorium... and no, I didn't make the hearse stop off at The Gower. I was in residence and yes, my not staying at the house did cause comment but then blowing your nose in the street does that round here.

Mother's friend, Enid Williams, and that fat ugly daughter of hers are staring at me over the heads. It's not what you'd call a mining village, you know - Mother would have torn a strip of skin off anyone calling it a mining village – but the people in these parts are still pretty short. I found that out when I moved to London. I went from being average height in the local girls' school to the midget of Finsbury Park.

I must say the old house is looking good ... my house, now, of course - that's what they're all thinking: Mother's quality pieces of Regency-retro gleaming in the wide Edwardian room, legs reflected in the parquet floor - and the sun setting at the end of a half-acre garden... everything well-ordered, uncluttered ... and nothing like the patterned-carpet-and-ornaments that most of this lot go home to. Not a comfortable house, they might concede, but ... well ... tasteful.

Mother's room's very much along the same lines - watercolours of the Brecon Beacons, eau-de-nil walls, clothes hung or folded in the Waring and Gillow suite. Evan and Marcy had her safely stowed in the Chapel of Rest by the time I got here so I didn't have her lying in state while I went through the drawers ... hardly an attractive image, I know but it's not what it seems. I just wanted to get a head start on the detail...I mean, I'd every intention (I'd promised Duncan!) of being on that six-fifteen tonight.

It was the usual stuff - the will (I get the house and the bank account but I knew all that) and a complete biography of her Cambridge blue Metro (a handy gift, that's destined to be, for Evan and Marcy 'for all you've done'). A dental appointment for a month's time was predictably poignant as was the T.V. license bought only last week and the packets of seeds, safe in the airless dark of their lacquered tea-caddy, waiting for Spring... There were insurance policies to cushion the financial blow of death, subsidence, flooding, burglary, fire and storm and even vets bills and receipts for 'FEMALE CAT, NEUTERED, CLEO', one item I'm determined not to inherit.

The renewal of her BUPA membership made me grimace (a lot of good that did when the heart-attack struck) ... and it was then I found the cards - boxes and boxes of cards.

Greetings cards.

There were cards for every eventuality: Christmas cards, Birthday cards, Easter cards, Get Well cards and - worst of all - Mothers' Day cards. Truly dreadful cards. Giant cards. Vulgar and garish cards. There were cards with thatched cottages drenched in glitter and icicles. Cards featuring baby rabbits with real bits of ribbon round their necks, each tied in a bow. Big, padded cards where roses in sickly pink bulged out like blisters - or birds in violent blue-and-yellow satin hung upside down from a very green branch.

And who were they from, these treasured mementoes? Well, from me, so it seemed.

'To the best Mother in all the World, from Elizabeth with love'. 'Happy Birthday, Darling Mummy, from Elizabeth with all my love'. 'Have a Wonderful Christmas, Mummy! Can't wait to be home! Elizabeth'.

There they were in what appeared to be my handwriting - but then Mother and I have very similar hands: both upright and even. Hers you can tell because it has more loops while mine is pretty utilitarian. This writing was a hybrid: straight and clear above the line but with that strange curl on the y's and flourish on the zed's giving it away.

Not a bad forgery.

I flicked through them again - some were better than others. Perhaps she'd got closer with practise. All in perfect condition, they were hard to date. 'To My Mummy on her Special Day from Elizabeth with kisses and hugs.' How old was that meant to be, for God's sake? Kisses and hugs! Kisses and hugs? They could only have happened before I was three... isn't that when memory begins?

And there was I for the next twenty years thinking: Well, there's no love lost between us, as they say around here, but at least we understand each other.

Waiting for Perestroika

They attacked early that morning. Five past ten we drew up at The Bay Horse car-park, opened the door and they were on us, half a dozen at least - some grossly fat - all trying to climb aboard. The van laboured on its suspension and the books shifted.

"You got us anything really nice, today, Sally?" said the first. "Anything new?"

"Well there's the latest Catherine Cookson," I said. I don't approve of blood sports and this was like tossing somebody's poor tabby to hounds.

"You got that? Where? I thought we 'ad to go on the list!"

Nothing could be said without excessive body-movement. The very frail old creature that had just heaved itself up the step was instantly lost at sea.

"Just joking," I said. "You might get a look at it ... oh, two thousand and three, or some time after."

Dot and her sister Megan - both built like Sumo wrestlers - cackled. It was a deep and excessively female noise. I bet either could've made a living giving phone sex, even in retirement.

"Oh, you madam. She's a mean little cow, that one! Isn't she a mean little cow, Meg?"

"Language, ladies," I said. "Anymore of that and I'll put you on a course of Antonia Fraser, all terribly genteel."

"Oh no, we don't want none of that - we don't want nothing too stuck up!"

"But," I couldn't help pointing out as I reclaimed the eight assorted romances, "most of this stuff is about..... about," I picked one at random, "Merial, the lovely but high-spirited daughter of an mining engineer inherits her father's diamond mine in Australia and comes into conflict with Nick Van Owen, the ruggedly handsome geologist who nevertheless-"

I flicked through its dog-eared pages. "She ran a thin white finger along the proud bones of his tortured face. "Oh, God,

Merial," he breathed, "Oh, God, Oh God, oh God! You're just too beautiful to touch!" The girl's hand dropped onto the fine silk of her dress just as his- oh for goodness sake! What a load of- I mean not exactly gritty realism, is it?"

"It was good, that one was," Megan said, "'is mam 'ad bin widowed when 'is dad's wagon went off the road late one night, nobody knew 'ow-"

"Hit a kangaroo, I suppose."

"-an he'd paid 'is own way through school an that was what made 'im a bit on the pushy side, you know."

"Don't tell me," I said, " he was a rough diamond."

Dot let out a shriek that set off the pub's Rottweiler, Ophelia. (Don't ask). "Take no notice of 'er, our Megan," Dot said. "She's just windin' you up. In your face, she is today."

"Where do you two pick it up this jive-talk? Thank-god for Mills and Boon. They keep you inside and off the streets... otherwise you'd be out goosing old men and selling glue to poor teenagers."

"No," said Megan, "that's where you're wrong Miss Clever-Knickers. We'd be out goosing young men and selling our favours."

"Bloody 'ell," said her sister, "We'd be bankrupt then."

And all this was the day Dan came in and said something I never expected to hear in the back of the travelling library.

"What have you got by Solzhenitsyn, please? I'll need them all but Cancer Ward would do for a start."

It was just so right: his face as pale as a chronic invalid's, his eyes glittering in the gloom as Alexander Pushkin's were said to glitter when he gave a reading.

"Well the short answer is, I've got none ... not here. I can get them for you. If you'd like to order them I can-"

"Don't you bother, boy," Dot interposed, fingering his arm, making it clear they were all acquainted, "I say, Megan, tell Dan 'ere not to bother orderin' stuff off this one. Tell 'im Meg."

"Oh, that's right! Don't be doin' it. Twenty-two weeks she 'ad me waiting for *Passion in Paradise*. Twenty-two weeks! I bet it didn't take the girl that long to write the bloody thing."

"I bet it's not a girl, " I said, stamping the new batch she had chosen with unnecessary force. "All this stuff's churned out by a bloke called Brian, living in Basingstoke... a great big scruffy ex-policeman with ginger hair coming out of his nose." Megan and Dot glared. "Brian," I said, "he's Sonia Logan, Marianne Clark and," I banged Meg's final selection on top of the heap "and this, er, Ginetta Gale. All Brian from Basingstoke, every one."

"Twenty-two weeks," said Megan, "an' then when I got it some kid 'ad scribbled all over the back page."

"There you go, then," said her sister. "See you next week, Sally love."

The springs wheezed their relief.

"Do you know those two?"

"Yes." When he smiled he looked less unusual, less intense. "I'm the new tarecake- caretaker, at their flats, you know?"

"Oh yes, I know. They're my best customers. In fact, mostly they're my only customers. Sometimes, when I get back to Mold, with the van, and I've done all these villages and I've issued all these romances and bodice-rippers and Jeffrey Archers and whodunnits - Winnie, the er, the fat lady - the fattest lady - very into murders, she is, gorier the better... anyway, I've done all this and I think, something must've happened out there. They've slapped an enormous tax on reading, you know, five pounds per book or whatever, and nobody told me ... oh, yes, but they've exempted pensioners ... that's why Grey Girl Power out there are the only ones can afford it."

"To order the books ... ?" he prompted.

"No problem. I'll get you *Cancer Ward* and *The First Circle* for next week. I have this hunch they'll be available. You'll have to join the library. Just fill this in."

Daniel Jenkyn, I watched him write, The Annex, Ffrith House, Graig. He laid it down very carefully and then lined up his Council Identity Card so that they just touched.

Just touched. It took him two attempts.

"Great, that's great. I'll get you a ticket made. See you next week, Daniel."

"Dan," he said, "It's just Dan. Thank-you ... um."

Bad sign. Three chances, at least, and he hadn't picked up my name.

A week later I had the collected works of Solzhenitsyn under the counter. It doesn't do to look too keen. There was Dan, helping old Miss Roberts back down onto terra firma, clutching Jacqueline Suzanne's *Valley of the Dolls* - again. I suspect she just couldn't believe some of the things described the first time around.

Megan and Dot - and I - watched him depart with with every word Alexander Isayevich Solzhenitsyn had committed to print.

"Studying," said Dot. "Open University."

"Oh yes," said the other, "up early and the telly on all hours at night."

"How do you know?"

"Oh, she can see in from 'er flat, isn't that right Meg? Specially if she leans out of the bathroom window with 'er feet tucked under the wash-basin and 'as 'er distance glasses on".

"You're a disgrace," I told them and "Keep off! He's mine."

For the first time ever Dot turned serious on me. She returned my look but not my smile. She had irises the colour of a stagnant pond – a deep stagnant pond.

"Stray dogs, Sally love."

"Mm?'

"It's what our old mam said - when I was a kid. Watch out for stray dogs, they always snap."

Out in the pub yard, Ophelia started up.

I didn't see him for a while. My employers in their lack of wisdom sent me to a series of 'Violence at Work' seminars (which did not equip me to eject smelly old men off the van with a single, neat flick of the wrist). Whoever renewed Dreamy Dan's set texts when they were due, it wasn't me ... and then, one morning, there he was: his face paler if anything, his hair longer, his fingers tapping an irritable Morse message while he waited his turn.

"Hello," I said, "how are things in the former Soviet Union?"

"Very interesting."

"You'll want all of these, again?"

"Yes, if that's O.K. I'm still working on Marxism, Character and Culture," he said self-importantly ... and he did something horrible: he grinned... no, he smirked. The young Martin Amis - the one with all his own teeth - had just vanished before my eyes.

Folding my arms across a broken heart, "Why don't I get you *Dr Zhivago?*" I said.

"It's a film."

"Yes, a film of a book. Just because it's a film doesn't mean to say it can't be a great book as well. I mean he got the Nobel Prize-"

"Solzhenitsyn did."

"Yes, but so did Boris Pasternak."

"Who? "

"Pasternak... a revolutionary writer - except that he wasn't, I don't think. Loads of character and culture and not much Marxism but then it was probably safer that way ... I mean, who are we to judge? Stalin, Beria-"

"But Solz-synetshin-" now Dan was struggling over a name he'd pronounced perfectly every other go, "Solz-hen-itsyn ... he's the master, right? That's what it said ... in the notes - the module notes. The master Russian novelist."

"Well he is... a master. I'm just saying that there are others. Dostoevsky, Tolstoy-"

"No-o! I don't want to..in here there's everything... look ... look. "

He grabbed *August 1914* off the very inadequate counter that separated us. (Employers I recalled from my violence course have a duty to ensure the safety of staff by the manipulation of the physical environment. Where was my panic button and my armour-plated security glass ... where was my Group Four mace-wielding personal minder? Didn't the Council understand it was the front line out here in the travelling library van?)

"Look," Dan shouted, his pale-but-interesting face the colour of the *Writers and Artists' Year Book* - well the red bits.

I did look - in horror at the passage he was pointing to. The little swine had magic-markered it and there was a great big asterisk at the top of the page. Completely unselfconsciously he began to read:

"'This was an emergency worse than a fire or a flood; at moments like this officers were useless - a sergeant-major with two brawny arms was what was needed. For all their generations of book-learning, officers could only cough apologetically when there was man's work to be done.' See? There it is. The whole of the class-struggle summed up in those few words."

Did I mention he had this wonderful voice? Anthony Hopkins with a bit of rough? Still ...

"You've defaced it," I said.

"Oh, that, I just ... just noted it for my essay. But you see what

I mean? You don't have to know everything to get to the heart of it. I can't read all these others you're going on about. I've left it too late. But it doesn't matter... I can see what-"

Empires may wax and wane, tyrannies rise and be bloodily put down but we ... well, we're still waiting for perestroika in the literature-lending lark.

"I'm sorry," I said, "but mutilating books is a very serious matter."

I thought of Joe Orton and his lover (what was his name?) and their lengthy guerrilla war against publicly owned volumes everywhere - but I kept my expression bland. Never, they had stressed on the course, allow these things to become personalised. "The library service may require payment to cover the cost of the damage and... or may cancel the borrower's ticket. "

Dan snatched up his Solzhenitsyns. "Excellent," he said. "Outstanding! When I bring these back ... when I've finished my essay, well you can just chop off my hands ... or, or gouge my eyes out. How about that? Or you could just stick your library stamp up where the sun don't shine."

He jumped down the steps and ran off as though he expected someone to give chase and wrestle him to the ground over a few grubby hardbacks and one Penguin Modern Classic. When he'd gone I couldn't really tell if it was the van that kept on shaking or if it was me.

Halliwell - Michael, Lesley ... Kenneth? - Joe Orton's lover.

Killed him in a fit of rage.

I knew he'd come back.

But I never saw my hero, Dan - or the Solzhenitsyns - again. He did return to the travelling library but it was a couple of months later and I was off with the flu. The new, gormless woman they'd just taken on was doing the rounds and of course Dot and Megan were there to see it all.

"Oh, yes," said Dot, her thin lips saying 'shame' while her wicked old eyes rolled with remembered pleasure and excitement. "Terrible it was ... jumped up 'ere 'e did, never a word to that poor girl you'd sent Sally."

"I didn't send her," I protested.

"Jumped on the van," said Megan, "an' just starts throwing the books off. All of them. Great armfuls of books ... sweeps them up and chucks them onto the car-park. Wet it was too, wasn't it?"

"Oh wet - we'd had nothing but rain... all those lovely books lying in puddles and then, Dan, he goes an' he sits down with 'em and starts tearing out the pages. Ophelia's going ber-r-serk and him cryin' like a kid. Sobbin' fit to break your heart...it did upset us," she finished with relish.

"Back in hospital, they say," said her sister.

"Back?"

She didn't want to own up to not having known. "Best place, really. All that studying, it must've turned 'is brain."

I stamped eight assorted tales of big moustaches and lust repressed in Edwardian England and handed them over in silence.

"The police came you know?" Dot persisted, "a man and woman. Pretty little thing. Swearin' he was, by then. A real to-do. Twice over he used the f-word."

"What, fines?" I said. "I don't think I'll be seeing any of them."

Waste Flesh

When Vinny came home and turned the corner into Melidan Street, just for a second he saw it as a stranger might: two rows of identical dolls' houses psyching each other out across a strip of new tarmac. The council must've made it No Parking because there was a brace of acid-yellow lines now painted on top. Gary Bithel's old Norton 500 was breaking them up across from Vinny's Mam and Dad's.

The Crawfords, two doors down, had been pebble-dashed as a late riposte to the Flynns' stuck-on stone ... while Mam and Dad ... oh, shit! Mam and Dad had new white plastic windows with diamond-shaped leaded-lights and the excess mortar still coating some of the old Ruabon bricks like badly applied coffee icing.

Once Vinny started thinking about the people who lived there the street clicked back into its old remembered form. He couldn't really see it anymore. Eighteen years opened up the buildings, spewing out their inhabitants, past and present, the Bithels, Vaughans, Crawfords, Lanes, Wynns, Flynns - and himself and parents at different ages ... so that when Number Six really did open and Gaynor Flynn stepped in front of him with kids and a big mongrel dog on a chain and a black bin bag clutched in her bare, round arm he felt crowded.

"'ello Vinny," she said, "- not more bloody 'olidays, is it?"

Gaynor was only a year or so older than Vinny and to hear her talking in the tones of Grandma Crawford while her bright hair shone like a torch against the dark interior gave Vinny the instant blues.

"That's right. Easter vac."

He watched her take in his new goatee, well-worn boots and the camera slung about his neck. "Lucky sod."

"I know."

"You photographing all them top models yet?"

"No. Not interested in fashion."

"Oh I can see that ... well just you let me know when you want me to pose Vinny .... get my kit off, yes?"

"I will."

"Yeah - you let me know when ... and I won't be in."

The little group made off at Gaynor's brisk pace with only the dog turning to look back at him. Regretful, it seemed.

Vinny had to knock at his own home because his key wouldn't fit the unfamiliar mahogany-panelled monstrosity.

"Hi, Mam. Bit of a change, huh?"

"I know. Kept it as a surprise - that's what your Dad said to do. D'you like it?"

"No."

"What d'you mean, no? Cost three thousand pound that did, what with security locks throughout and the bit of stained glass. Look at that!" Vinny's Mam made the door pivot to catch the late-afternoon light. "Look at that. Red tulips - see the red on the wall? Lovely they are. Your Dad wanted roses - you know, for the Labour - but they didn't have none in stock."

"It could've been worse, then."

"Oh, so you've come back a Tory, this time?" His Mam couldn't stop playing with the coloured refractions ... back and forth, back and forth as though she were being hypnotised by them - or trying to hypnotise her son. "D'you 'ear that Col? Doesn't like the new door and he's pining for Benny Potts!"

Sir Benjamin Potts was the local Conservative, put in for years by the regiment of the retired living along the coast. The Bungalow Fascists, his Dad called them. Vinny could glimpse his Dad, now, at the far end of the house, eating at the kitchen table, framed by two doorways but offset to the left.

Radiance from an unseen source caught the pottery mug, the aluminium teapot, his big, pale hands. "'ello there," he called to Vinny in that odd tone he'd always brought out for greeting his son. It was the tone people used when they met someone they didn't really know for the second time.

Vinny's Dad was the handsomest man in North Wales - now that he'd travelled a bit, Vinny thought it might well be in the whole of Britain - this darkly dangerous James Dean with the brains not to kill himself before reaching forty-three. "Looking good, Dad."

His Dad nodded. The perfect lines of his face held sepia

shadows beneath brow and cheek-bones, so that whatever he did, wherever he went, he always managed to look like a movie star playing the part of husband, father, miner, union activist ... security guard.

"Catch you in a minute, Dad."

Vinny vaulted up the stairs and bashed his way into his room using the bag. A new plastic window with stick-on leaded lights looked out over the strip of dandelions and lawn. 'Last Shift at Point of Ayr', a two-by-four blow up, semi-matt finish, had fallen off the wall and lay rolled on the bed. Gently he unslung the old Canon Program and laid it on the quilt. In next door's garden Mrs Lane walked into shot shouting abuse at her hyperactive grandchild but no voice filtered through Vinny's double-glazed lens on the world.

Down in the kitchen while his mother washed lettuce and sliced cheese he said, "I've got this project to do. Photo-journalism, it's called. I thought I'd do this place. What d'you think?" He mimed the camera's focus and click, missing the familiar weight of the Canon against his breast-bone.

"What? How we've done it up, you mean? Like in one of those magazines?"

"Na ... not the house. The whole place." Vinny turned away so as not to have to catch her disappointment. "Thought I'd do a portrait of the ... er community. You know, the end of the Flintshire coalfield ... unemployment. Social problems ... decay. Vandalism."

"Oh well, if it's vandalism you want you better go to Rhyl. Wrecked the bus-shelter, they 'ave ... and paint - all up Undersea World! But I don't think you should be taking pictures of that. Just encourages them. Makes them think it's clever... and they're selling drugs in that little cafe me and your Dad did our courting in. Smack ... right opposite the Sun Centre."

"It'll be a few spliffs, Mam, if you've seen them at it."

"It's all drugs. You take their photos and these druggies think they're somebody."

"Mam if I started taking smackheads' pictures I'd end up in the Marine Lake."

"That's what I said," said his Mam.

"No," said Vinny, "it's not about deciding to make some things look important - that's not why ... I just want to show what's here

... there's the mine - or there was - which was work and the seaside which was ... well holidays, the opposite ... and this village, with no real reason to exist anymore."
"Oh, thanks very much."
"I didn't mean it like that."
He tried to make eye-contact with his Dad wanting to share some feeling about his Mam that he had no word for. "We have this tutor - he did a whole book on the Shotton Steel works when that went. Black and white - thirty-eight full-page bleeds using only natural light." His Mam stared uncomprehendingly.
"Sounds like it's all been done, then," his Dad said. "Been done to death, that sort of stuff...down South. Big thing, mining and steel was to them. They'd got nothing else at the time." Vinny tried not to smile: down South meant London to him. "Still haven't. Anyway, nice to see you back... I'm off up the road for a couple of hours - committee meeting ... keep an eye out for some social problems for you, shall I?" He was looking sharp - well-defined - in black denims and a blue shirt, which somehow made it sound even more ridiculous.
Vinny waited until the door slammed and sprinted upstairs. He was back out in the street in time to freeze his Dad against a bright grey sky. Gary had sportingly moved his wreck of a Norton and the bare terraces held the retreating figure - wide shoulders, straight back - as it sliced the horizon.
"You know," he said to his Mam who was still muttering on about how he mustn't mind his Dad, as though if both parents got into a who-could-get-furthest-up-your-nose competition, she wouldn't always be an outright winner.
"You know, it's really weird - eighteen years underground and Dad never got a stoop."
"Your grandad had a stoop," his Mam offered, "and tiny he was - only my height ... like a garden gnome, Colin used to say. I think he'd had rickets when he was a boy."
"But he's dead... and he was on the railway. He's no use. I can't photograph him."
He mulled it over while he cruised with the Canon, trying to work out what it was his Dad's silhouette brought to mind ... up Melidan and into Ash Grove catching an old woman in fluffy white clippers walking a Westie, wearing its relatives for the camera. Two boys sprawled across the bonnet of a parked car,

the smaller shouting "It's me brovers's an' 'e don't mind so piss off!" as Vinny snapped them.

He finished the film in the street: one of the Crawford girls rehanging her grandmother's net curtains, tom cats fighting on the footpath behind the scruffy strips of garden and a portrait of Les Lewis in his aviary with budgies fluttering about his head. Les had to clap to get them airborn and Vinny was allowed just one shot. "Doin' it more than once," said Les, " 'll leave the poor little buggers without a feather to their names."

Les's prize bird was called Tony after Tony Blair.

"Nice looker," Vinny ragged him, "but can he perform?"

Les was the Labour Party agent. He didn't rise. "You on the roll at y'Mam an Dad's?"

"Yeah, I guess ... on the roll but not on a roll."

Les wasn't interested in Vinny's problems. "Proxy vote is what you want, then, for the local elections. Those Liberal Democrats always sniffin' round, you know." He favoured a bright yellow bird with a vicious look. "Even that Plaid! And then there's this Assembly. Mind you, I reckon old Benny Potts won't live to run. Pickled."

Vinny grinned. Whatever his Mam said, booze remained the drug of choice round here.

"It's true! He could go at any time. Mervyn Price says he fears for the safety of the Crematorium if they get the job. Abide With Me - and then one hell of a big bang! Anyhow we don't want to get caught short and you off at that college. What you doin' there?"

"Photography ... with journalism. It's a sort of combined-"

"George Orwell," said Les, "he's the boy. Greatest journalist that ever lived. Got all his books upstairs ... if you want a lend."

"Thanks. Got most of them for A-level. Inside the Whale, Animal Farm, Nineteen Eighty-four ..." Vinny popped the lens-cap on: the only coda in his waking life. "I'll get these developed tonight. Bring you a copy of you and the birds, eh? I'm gonna put captions on them all, or a slice of text - 'Socialist attacked by true-blue budgies!'... 'Hitchcock comes to the arse-end of Flint!' "

Les turned away, his mind on millet. "Remind your Dad there's a committee meeting tomorrow. He's missed the last two."

He could've corrected Les but didn't. With people Les's age you could lose good time out of your allocation putting them right.

"You just keep watching the birdies," he said.

Vinny had to share his dark room with the Hoover, the ironing board and linen basket, a pile of old suitcases and a half-dismembered shopper-bike. His spine ached. His elbows needed to be pinned close to his sides to prevent damage. If he straightened up one of the stairs grazed the crown of his head.

Even before the print was out of the fixing bath Vinny's brain closed on what it had been ferreting around for: those two lines of black italics that he could thread across the page.

George Orwell.

It was as if the long-dead writer had lain in his grave, just waiting for Vinny Morris to capture the image of his words. 'Noble bodies' Orwell had said, 'wide shoulders tapering to slender supple waists' and 'not an ounce of waste flesh anywhere.' This was Orwell's picture of miners: confident, athletic beings, physiques made beautiful in the performance of masculine function.

Not an ounce of waste flesh.

In Vinny's picture Karen or Carly or Ceri Crawford - whatever her name was - fought with the veil of nylon lace on her grandmother's glass ... but next door the bedroom was uncurtained and Gaynor Flynn's plump arms wrapped the hard muscles of his Dad's torso and Gaynor Flynn's face hid itself in the hollow of his Dad's neck.

"Looking good, Dad," Vinny said.

"Today we have naming of parts"

"Need a ride. darlin' ?"

She looked up and down Queens Street.

Twenty minutes ago you could've walked across on people's heads, as her mum would say. Now it was all but empty ... a couple of dossers bedding down for the night in the black doorway of the Cannon Cinema and a big all-male group just turning the corner into Tontine Place.

All-male.

It was true what they'd said on the news that day, about all those extra men. Too many men in the eighteen to twenty-five age group - not enough woman to go round - a demographic glitch. That lot now, drunk and loud, just disappearing from sight, they'd probably been in there, where she'd been - in the club - in The Maroc Seven. Not getting lucky. Not making out. Not latching on to come narcoleptic seventeen year-old whose idea of a good time was a skinfull followed by two minutes machine-tooling up against her own front door. Oh, they were out there, these bespoke, female companions, and willing, so long as you didn't mind them throwing up when you were half-way through, but there just weren't enough of them to go round - not at The Maroc Seven - not anywhere.

As she turned and looked at the flowing purple script of the neon sign, it went out.

"Right, darlin', what's it to be? I got a livin' to earn, you know."

He had a round, eager face, jaundiced by the street lights. The car was big but old, dark red by the looks of it. A white panel on the driver's door said SOMETHING-CABS. Afterwards she wouldn't be able to remember... WALSH CABS, WELSH, WALLIS? Her subconscious would keep on telling her it was WALES - WALES CABS, but that couldn't be right. That didn't sound right.

"Gomer Street? Can you take me to Gomer Street? It's out beyond The Infirmary, off St David's Road?"

"Course I can. Hop in - cost you a tenna."

She slid into the car's interior and had the familiar smell hit her in the back of the throat, that hospital smell of old vomit and synthetic pine. It had to be synthetic - there weren't enough pine trees in the world to cover the compound reek of humanity that she helped process ... and that was mainly men. Accident and emergency was always full of men - men and children ... and weren't they predominately boys? She hadn't noticed until now but it did seem that even at an early age, the males were burning, cutting, breaking and bruising themselves at a disproportionate rate. Burning, cutting, breaking and bruising ... first themselves, then other people.

Whereas she - she was just hammered.

No wonder she'd had that row with Gareth. She was so bloody weary every part of her was sensitive, every touch, every word could cause pain. It was like shingles of the soul ... in that foul club, going to relieve herself but really just wanting to get out of the noise, she'd stood and tried to do her hair in the smeared glass and it hurt to pull the comb across her scalp and it hurt to examine her own face.

Gareth knew the hours she worked. Birthday or no sodding birthday, couldn't he have found somewhere else to take her? He'd be back in a minute, she guessed - contrite but not wanting to show it. Back with his Hugh Grant smile - ready just to start talking again, so long as there was no postmortem. He'd be back, he'd be ready but she'd be gone.

"Had a good night, then?"

"What? Oh, not really - not in the mood."

She cursed herself for having chosen the wrong side of the seat. The driver was nicely positioned to catch her reflection, she realised, and since she didn't have a full facial birthmark and a hump had decided to go for it.

"What you do, then?"

"I work at the hospital ... The Infirmary." She hadn't meant to add this but the blue sign had just registered with her overworked brain and it had provided the line without being asked.

"Oh, a nurse!"

Oh, a nurse. First prize he made it sound like.

She had a hatred these days of telling anyone she was a

doctor. It wasn't just the freebies for minor complaints they expected - it was the horror stories that they all had polished up and ready to recount: the uncle left to peg out on a trolley, the misdiagnosed friend-with-a-lump. All the fault of doctors, these early deaths. Whereas the nurses, well, everyone knew they were angels weren't they? Underpaid, rushed off their feet, holding hands with the dying even as some white-coated sadist carved up the patients before they were properly out.

She stayed silent.

"A nurse! I bet there's not much shocks you, eh? I bet you see some sights!"

"Uh-huh."

"I'll bet you do. See everything, you do."

They swerved to avoid a car-door, flung open, a drunk being decanted not onto the pavement but onto the road. Minor cuts and abrasions to the palms, knees and face by the looks of it. Suturation needed above the left eye.

Potentially abusive and/or violent.

Three friends, ditto.

"Is it true what they say about nurses? Is it?"

She didn't reply. She looked down at her hands clenched around the ridiculously small bag, her fingers on the clasp shaped into a long brass fox.

A Present From Gareth.

She could feel the urgent gaze in the mirror - could feel, even, the dirty grin forming, which the mirror couldn't possibly show.

"They say that you nurses are real goers, you know? Goers, you know, like Harley-Davidsons. Legs apart, ninety miles an hour!"

It wasn't just the words - she heard worse in her job nearly every day. No - she heard much worse each day, now. A constant, repetitive stream... for today we have naming of parts. Today and tonight and every other shift, today, ladies and gentleman, bitches and wankers, today we have naming of parts. The words were an irritant, a stimulus to anger and then boredom, not fear. So why was an alarm sounding deep inside her exhausted self?

That sign - the sign that said INFIRMARY. There should have been two: the first at traffic lights, the second at the roundabout. There should have been two but they'd passed only one because somewhere the cab had taken a wrong turning - and now when she searched for the familiar little shops and Edwardian terraces they'd disappeared. A lorry park loomed into view, its sleeping monsters clustered around a single harsh beam, and beyond that lay the blackness of waste ground.

"Oh, yes, real goers, you nurses," he whispered.

The cab slowed and began to turn in a long shallow arc that sent them bumping and rocking away from the deserted road. Even before trying them, reason told her that both doors would be locked. Child-proofed - as though the darkness were infested by hoards of rampaging children from which the car's passengers might need protection.

He killed the engine and snuffed out the lights.

"You know, darlin'," he said, "I don't get it - a clever girl like you, dressed like that - tits falling out, skirt up to your arse. Goin' about on your own at this time of night. Askin' for trouble. All the same, you little cunts. Askin' for everything you get. You'd think you'd be too scared.... aren't you scared?'

"No," she said wearily - and it was just then he felt the scalpel blade prick the newly shaven skin beneath the his jaw.

"No," she said, "but you should be."

Mercer Preece (R.A.?) R.I.P.

"It's getting like Norfolk round here," Meryl said.
Her cousin's ancient Volvo was grinding its way up Moel Graig to a cottage perched above the Vale of Clwyd. Its huge grey stones had been amongst those once worked for the Roman outpost that guarded a Celt-infested pass.
"What? Flat, you mean?"
"Ha-bloody-ha! No, you know what I mean. That's the last craft fair I do. Everywhere's touristy...full of couples from Kent who want a nice little view of some waterfall." To add emphasis to her complaint, a stack of bubble-wrapped, aluminium-framed prints leapt off the back seat as the car hit a rut. When Meryl shot out a hand to steady them, they opened up like a deck of cards, brilliantly coloured as though each were royalty.
"Bastards, huh?" said Hannah. "Shooting's too good for them, if you ask me ... Hey! Your sign's taken a hit."
On the road lay a green board : Tŷ Meryl, Gallery and Art Shop, Paintings, Pottery, Object d'art, Handmade paper, Books.
Across the white gothic lettering black tyre tracks were clearly visible.
"I suppose this is what they mean by passing trade," Meryl said.
The two women got out and dragged the sign and splintered post onto the grass verge. "Come in for a drink for God's sake, Han, or I'll have to open my veins." Silently they unloaded the unsold prints and a collection of bizarre pots.
"Is this one broken?" Hannah querried searching the car floor by touch.
"No," Meryl said, "it isn't."
"Oh, so it never had a handle?"
"No, it did not."
Hannah said, not quite under her breath, "I thought old Joyce had popped her clogs."
"She has."

"And you're still trying to flog these ... these glazed cowpats?"

"I had them on sale or return," said Meryl. "Who am I going to return them to now?"

The interior of Tŷ Meryl was so untidy the living room had the appearance of mere storage space for the adjacent business. Hannah lowered herself onto one of the Georgian milking stools a local joiner had been knocking out for over a year . There was no other resting place. Unopened boxes occupied both chairs and a small sofa. Hannah glared. Meryl followed her eyes.

"Oh it's copies of Weird Wales by that mad-looking bloke, runs the DIY. I've been selling twenty copies a week since the Abergele UFO. Scotch or lager?"

"A gin and tonic would be nice."

"Scotch it is then," Meryl said and brought doubles.

For Hannah there was an extra something - a small watercolour, its mount slightly marked, its frame well-worn gesso. The subject was simplicity itself: a single-story thatched cottage overborn by a fine horse chestnut. A pale sky and uncluttered background seemed to stretch away in every direction - as though the little scene were a glimpse of a larger, emptier planet. It was signed but Hannah had to carry it to the window and only then could she make out "Mercer Preece".

"It's er...nice, Meryl," the older woman breathed. "Have you any idea as to where it is?"

"Oh yes. It's Graig Cross, around eighteen-sixty, before the railway came. Will it go in the shop?"

The shop was down on the main road - Hannah's horribly successful Hen Bethau (meaning 'ancient stuff', the Welsh lacking the concept of wormy old chairs being worth money when they were putting their language together). "Oh, yes," Hannah said, and "how much?"

"A couple of hundred ... if you knock off my share of the petrol."

"Done ... mm, Mercer Preece, Mercer Preece ... and you got it?"

"Never mind," Meryl said.

Only when she'd seen her cousin safely on her way, did she risk opening up the studio. Five boards sat with their ready stretched paper. On two just the background washes in well-watered prussian-blue were in place whilst the other three showed patches of greenery and some raw umber details on buildings or cottage walls. To every board there was clipped a curled sepia photograph. Some long-dead but obliging hand had written a location on each of them in Indian ink: Moel Graig in Winter, The Old Smithy in Tegid Lane, Ploughing Team at Eglwys Farm, The River Dee At Graig and (Meryl's especial favourite) Miss Nia James at Dolphin House, Pantypont.

Miss Nia James looked a real Tartar - stern, upright - a relentless fortysomething virgin - and her cousin Hannah's doppleganger if ever there was one. Meryl, captured by the image, sat down at the end board and began work on Miss James' drab, grey dress. It was a shade of which Hannah was particularly fond.

The way these people circulated their spruced-up junk, she might need to take this one as far down as Ludlow to offload it. She didn't want it fetching up in Hen Bethau. Hannah had the sort of character that made a Jack Russell look a bit casual, if not downright complacent. Two hundred here and maybe three there'd prove a timely solution to Meryl's current money worries - but not if her Lovejoy-like cousin were syphoning off half ... especially now Mercer Preece, that rare, masterly, undervalued, Victorian, non-existent watercolourist was experiencing a revival in Meryl's studio.

By the end of the month all five paintings were complete and mounted in a selection of old frames bought at car boot sales all over North Wales. Each had endured a very slight distressing and an afternoon under an elderly sunlamp of lethal, cancer-producing design. With a fine patina of dust (courtesy of the Hoover bag) Meryl slid them onto the market,one per fortnight. Offloading Hannah (alias Miss Nia James) to a slick little chap in Shrewsbury proved both exhilarating and educational.

"The subject, um?"

"Dolphin House," Meryl offered helpfully. "A Palladian-style dower house long gone, of course. Dreadful shame, isn't it? Probably a car-park now..." It was actually her local Tescos but it didn't do to supply too much free info.

"Mercer Preece - well, a complete unknown I'm afraid dear. Not R.A. - that's Royal Academy - as far as I'm aware. Nice... ish as a decorative object. Maybe fifty pounds-"

"I'm trade," said Meryl.

He was unabashed. "Two-twenty, but that's top end."

"Two-fifty," Meryl countered. "There's a Preece in Chester this week going for three-seven-five. Smaller than this, too."

"Oh, size isn't everthing, duckie!"

"It is when it comes to art. Three-seven-five. I kid you not."

It was only the truth, as far as Meryl knew it. In fact Ploughing Team at Eglwys Farm was at that moment on its way to Kentucky with an American bloodstock breeder and his bleached-blonde third wife. The heavy horses and harness had proved the devil's own work but the painting's new owners were more than appreciative. Cindy (an ex-rodeo rider) just 'lurved those darlin' old-fashioned legs'.

He surrendered with a sigh and Meryl pocketed her notes.

"Actually," he said giving a questionable secretaire a buff and so avoiding her eyes. "I've a couple of...interested parties down in London if you come across anything similar."

It was strange the way Mercer Preece sold. While Meryl's own flashy, vibrant prints travelled from library to art shop to town hall and back to Tŷ Meryl without laying a glove on any passing connoisseur's wallet, a Mercer Preece always moved the moment it was dry. The temptation to do just one more, although fiercely resented by her painter's ego, grew. It proved irresistable in the face of the bottled-gas supplier's desire that money should change hands now and again...and Mercer Preece himself became a fascinating character, his artistic development something to manage and observe with pride.

Born around eighteen-thirty, Meryl determined ... a highly convenient time since, as every local schoolchild knew, the Great Graig Flood (and landslip) of eighteen-seventy had carried away the ancient church of St Urith and all its records. An only child ... self-taught ... but not entirely, having had a drawing master as a boy. Meryl's own skills in line and perspective - something considered almost shameful at The Slade - proved the utility of this early training.

The first half-dozen Preeces were, of course, a young man's work. They were precise and pleasing but overly deferential to the Thomas Girton - seventeen seventy-five to eighteen oh-two - school. It came as great relief to Meryl when her protege fell under the liberating influence of Joseph Mallord William

Turner, adopting the old man's use of light to tell the story of landscape and reflection to conjure up form. In fact he must have trodden quite literally in the master's footsteps, painting many of the his chosen subjects - at a slightly different angle.

'Caernarvon Castle from the River' hovered, delicate as sugarwork above the lemon and white water, as a pair of naked youths struck out for the drifting boat and a golden horse drank. Sunshine lifted off the best quality paper in a continuous stream to gild the face of a potential purchaser. It was a wonderfully successful endeavour combining a morning's work in the July heat followed by lunch and a leisurely walk round the shops.

It sold to a Manchester dealer for five-hundred and twenty pounds, no questions asked.

In the autumn she took Mercer Preece on a tour of the coast. They stayed at little hotels where the rambling-rose carpets clashed with print curtains in shades beloved by Gaugain

"A painter? Oh, well," their host in Abersoch (a Mr Pitt from Bromsgrove) became instantly solicitous, "you'll be after views then. You should go for a walk along the sand towards The Warren, smashing it is ... y'know, picturesque." And it certainly must have been...before the caravan site. Even screwing her eyes up till she resembled Monet without his glasses couldn't make that disappear.

"You don't know the half of it, mate," Meryl muttered to Mercer Preece as she struggled with easel and box back along the beach. "All you had to do was turn up and someone had put out a mountain, a moor, a tumbled-down cottage and a couple of milkmaids with their skirts tucked into their knickers. You could get straight to it, no worries."

An elderly, dog-walking couple gave her a nervous glance.

But ... Bardsey Island sportingly emerged from the mist just long enough to be captured as a shiny, floating pebble beneath the ghost of a sun - and the great scoop of Hell's Mouth gave her Wind and Steam, if not a lot of Speed.

She returned with five paintings and sold them all before Christmas. Mercer Preece appeared to promise a prosperous new year.

"You've changed your car," said Hannah. Meryl didn't recall asking her for Boxing Day but she'd turned up just the same.

"Well, you know, I'm teaching that night class down at the

school." (It was true) "And... the shop's had a good year.' (It was not).

"Oh, there's nice."

Hannah savoured the rich, October, Gallic festival of calvados on her tongue and regarded Meryl's well-stocked drinks cabinet.

"That little watercolour you did me for..."

"Which one was that?" Meryl busied herself with the grapes and tangerines in the fruit bowl, as though setting up for a still life.

"Preece ... yes, Mercer Preece, I think it was ... not in the window a week. I remembered because of the initials. M.P. you know. Meryl Paine ... Mercer Preece. No reference to him in The Bulletin ... I rang the Museum of Wales."

"Really?"

There was just a small cluster of detached grapes that Meryl tried fitting into various valleys and caverns of citrus. Each time they self-ejected.

Exasperated she flopped down opposite her cousin, stripped them from their stalk and popped them into her mouth, letting the sharp juices stream down her throat as they burst. "Well," she drawled - chomp, chomp - "I didn't say he was anybody..."

"No," said Hannah, "and at a few hundred quid no one's going to get all forensic, are they?"

"Wouldn't be," chomp, chomp, "likely," Meryl agreed.

"In fact, these days I bet nobody'd bother to check for anything less than ... nine hundred... ?" Hannah speculated.

"Six to seven-fifty," Meryl countered, "to be...to be totally sure it wouldn't be worth any nosy sod's- any interested collector's while."

"My own thoughts exactly! You - em - you haven't come across ... you know... any more? By the same artist?"

"Mm. Funny you should mention it! Only the other day...little ink-and-wash job. Evening - The Menai Straits. Exquisite. Perfect lines and just the two pigments added - Burnt Sienna and Ultramarine - or at least that would be my guess."

As an old man Mercer Preece must have rediscovered the delights of draughtsmanship - that skill nurtured long ago in his boyhood in Graig.

"Signed?" Hannah demanded.

"Initialled."

"Ah, nice. Dated?"

"Don't be bloody daft..... paper's aged, though, quite ... noticeably."

Hannah nodded wisely. "Only to be expected, I mean these things were often badly treated and if you're keen on a bit of Victoriana you're not talking mint condition. Shall we say one-thirty?"

"Oh, I think one-fifty."

Hannah sighed. She knocked back her liqueur. "I'll be taking it, shall I? Oh, there's a nuisance! No chequebook."

Meryl managed a smile as she handed over the danegeld.

"That's fine. It is Christmas... I give a discount for cash... however small the amount."

She hadn't meant to come to the Hollins Hall sale... not up until the very last minute. These country house auctions were not worth the effort and poor indicators of the current market. Too much dodgy gear seeding a few, genuine, cokehead-aristos cast-offs. Too many punters having a day out - in the belief they'd pick up an unrecognized Rembrandt and be ennobled by lottery-style wealth.

There were a few families picnicing on the terrace trying for free gawp at the Hall's famous dining room... even though according to Hannah its Sevres and Sheraton had been flogged off before World War Two.

Just the thought of Hannah had the acid in her stomach on the boil. When they came to the clothes she must look out something pretty and delicate for her cousin. Something with an infestation.

She drifted through the Great Barn under the rheumy gaze of a security guard old enough to be her grandfather. One thing was obvious. The Hollins family had been terribly afflicted with artistic females. Basically this legion of surplus women had painted anything that flew or grew. 'Natural history studies', the catalogue called them, 'charmingly executed by the Misses Katherine, Elizabeth and Mary Hollins during their-'

Meryl turned away in disgust ... viciously, flicked over the page-

The name Mercer Preece leapt out.

Lot Fifty-Two ... described as 'The Vale Of Dovey. A Watercolour - twenty-one by fourteen point nine centimetres. Signed by the artist.'

Hurriedly she sought it out amongst the kingfishers, fritillaries and pasty spring flowers.

The frame was right. The damp-damaged mount a bit over the top - the dirt under the glass cleverly introduced so that with judicious juggling the light would reveal an unsoiled painting free of any real blemish. The scene was well-chosen... soft, sylvan, rising gently to the left as a mass of cloud built in the far diagonal to balance the weight of the hills.

Alizarin Crimson suggested heather with a mere touch in the wet.

There was more.

A little ruin spilled its walls and cool slates toward the observer and against it lay ... my God! ... lay a barefoot, exhausted boy.

Meryl had never set eyes on that view in her life. And if she had she would have missed - oh, she was quite sure she would have missed - the possessions fallen from the hand of the drowsing child: the dirty crust, the lapwing's feather, the round, blue stone.

The Man Mill

Wales is an enormous country - or it was till somebody crumpled it up.
To get to see Menna (and Chloe and Nest) I had two choices: a thirteen mile drive (on single track roads) or a shortish walk. By shortish I mean as assessed from a helicopter. The climb was a thousand feet followed by an eight-hundred foot descent. To add interest, the down side held a field of slate-spoil. It kept it for just for that point in the trek when you felt you might be going to survive and the ravens of Creigiau Llwyd might be going without their tea (your battered, blood-soaked corpse).
No contest, you'd think, would you? Get the old Jeep out and in fifteen minutes you're safe and snug in the Rowlands' kitchen - except that you'd never get in.
That bloody Alternative Technology Centre's got a lot to answer for - all windmills and solar panels and cawl made out of lentils. That's fine, I told them, for Holland and California and whatever poor benighted place the Lentil Tree grows in, but for Wales? It's no bloody good for Wales. Anyone who can't see that has got ginseng poisoning. Our wind, Welsh wind, it's for leaning into when you're crossing the yard, and even then it can change direction or disappear so fast you're on your face or your arse. As for the sun, well that's for the holiday makers to take a quick snap of before the clouds boil up and it's 'who's for a sprint back to the car?'
Lentils? Look around you. See those grubby bits of cotton wool, each with four legs and a mouth, balanced on every rock ledge? I rest my case.
Just thinking about the three of them over there at Melin-y-ferched is enough to drive a man mad. The trouble with Menna and Nest (who are sisters) and Chloe (who is their cousin) is... Menna, Chloe and Nest. God you should see them. The sisters are fair but with dark eyes and Chloe has the eyes and hair to match. They've the same full lips, long necks, slim, sloping

shoulders - and there are three of them. This is the terrible thing. Get into that house, spend half an hour watching the trio walk, talk, move about, sit still, weave a path around the low stone-walled rooms - even when they ignore you altogether - and you're lost. If you went in thinking monogamy had anything to be said in its favour, you'd come out cured.

You couldn't want one. You couldn't have a favourite because that changed depending on how the light caught a touch of red in Chloe's hair or Menna laid her little white hand on your arm and said, "Glen, what you need is..."

Nest has this habit of running the tip of her tongue along her perfect teeth when she's thinking...

It was the waterwheel that did for me - that and the sweatlodge. They had this witless plan for cutting themselves off from the National Grid and going self-sufficient. A real Nobel-Prize winning idea this turned out to be. I mean, there were poles and coax strung for miles up the valley just so the free-range yoghurt stays fresh and these three airheads wanted to generate their own power.

"Exactly," said Menna.

"What?"

"If we have our own, they can take down all those wires and restore the valley to how it should look."

"It doesn't work like that."

"It should," said Nest.

"Once they've put it in, they don't take it out. It's like nobody tears a road up to plant a wood, do they? No. They'll leave the supply, even if you don't use it. Then some time in the future, when somebody sensible buys your farm, they'll be able to have a jacuzzi with the sheep of their choice and watch satellite T.V."

None of them laughed.

"Can you get the part for the wheel?" demanded Chloe.

"Of course not. You think they stock them at B and Q? I'd have to get it cast. It'll cost a bloody fortune ... even, then, well, I don't know. I'm an agricultural engineer. What you need is an archeologist."

It had been a long, frustrating day spent up to my knees in the mud of their would-be millpond.

Three pairs of eyes attended, stricken.

I must've slipped into my Creep of the Week act.

"Oh well, I might just get on to this bloke down in Conwy..."
"Yes!" said Chloe.
"That would be fantastic," said Nest.
"Sweat-lodge," said Menna and all of them stripped off their clothes.
Every stitch.
For the sweat lodge.
How to build a sweatlodge: you knock up this structure, right? Out of branches and any other bits the tree can spare. This one was made out of conifer trimmings they'd brought down from the plantation ... a bit prickly for my taste. As a structure it was a joke. To visualise it, all you need to do is think 'igloo' - but an ogloo run up in wood by a trainee Innuit who lacked the confidence to invest in real snow.

Obviously this had been their day's work. The fire pit for baking stones had died down to just approachable. They took it in turns with the metal tongs, tranferring the murderous gobbets of heat from outside to in.

You know that smart-alec thing about 'I like work. I can sit and look at it for hours'? If allowed, I could have spent the best years of my life just lying on the grass in their excuse for a paddock, smelling the goat-turds, watching Menna, Nest and Chloe glide back and forth: slim, well-muscled, self-assured. When Chloe dropped a stone the scent of the earth singeing drifted across with its memory of years ago and my mother's burnt seed-cake.

They weren't perfect. Nest had a small scar where they'd taken out her appendix, Menna a birthmark on one hip. None of them shaved under their arms, which is something I'm usually strict on but ... but ... well, I don't know. How often does life offer anything like that?

That's as much detail as you're having. What do you expect? Half my lottery ticket?

I got naked. We all went inside. They explained about the sweat lodge and Native Americans which made me nervous on the embarrassment front - I mean I was up for a bit of chanting if need be but magic mushrooms were out. I was starting on Maxwell's combine-harvester at eight next morning. I didn't fancy hallucinations with my arm up its fanny. But it was fine. A sweat lodge turned out to be a medieval sauna.

Then a dip in the stream.

You'll've gathered that this is summer - last summer to be exact. I can remember getting out of the Christmas-tree igloo and running for the clear spring, enjoying being cool again not wanting to stand up because I knew the sun would have me dry and baking in ten minutes tops.

What I wouldn't give for those ten minutes now.

Of course 'we three' outlasted me in the steam... then out, sneering so as I'd know I hadn't quite measured up but by this time they were in the water, two long golden bodies and a paler one, that lay down beside me.

"So," Chloe said, "you know this bloke down in Conwy, do you? And you and Conwy Man are going to mend our wheel? Is that it?"

Another good thing about the stream that I forgot to mention: once in people can't see you dribbling.

"I'll see what I can do. But it's you er-" I wanted to say girls but we'd already had that conversation and it wasn't nice. How can anyone call them women? I'm thirty, right? Not exactly grandad material, but to me woman are what you see on the news: women have two kids and a pushchair and are out protesting at some accident blackspot next to a school.

"It's you I'm thinking of. I can't see it being cheap."

"That's O.K." Nest said, "we, um," she did that thing with her tongue and her teeth, "Yes, we'll get the money from the last exhibition through any day now."

Like I said - not perfect. Artists, they called themselves. Never any painting going on, of course, just a few bits of old twig and leaf, some copper wire and some sacking - stuck down, framed up and given a title.

"You sold much, have you?"

They all looked at each other and then at me. "A bit," Menna said.

"Even that one you did with the birch bark that stood up on its own? The one that-"

"Oh, yes," Nest giggled, "even that one."

"You know the third best thing about being in here?" said Chloe, "you can wet yourself and no-one would know."

That's what she said. Honest to God. 'The third best thing.' To go after my second best.

Witches, all of them.

It was time to turn the talk to something I knew about. Where we lay fifteen feet of wheel towered above us. She was beautiful too. There I was - half in, half out of the water with four handsome females.

"You need one new arm - at least - and maybe a couple of new flaunches," I told them. "What you have there is a breastshot wheel fed by a leat."

"You wouldn't be making this up, now, would you Glen?" Menna murmured.

Looking it up, that's what I'd been doing so I didn't have to go on ad libbing. "All true," I said.

"Even the bit about breasts?" the others laughed and turned onto their stomachs so that two pairs free-floated in the current.

"Of course. It means the water hits your wheel at axle-height ... it's a bit more unusual."

"Oh ... unusual. Unusual we like," Chloe said.

"I guessed."

"So you'll be getting the parts," Menna persisted, "the flaunches - you'll be getting them done? What are they anyway?"

"They're the things that look like the ace of clubs ... they hold the arms - the spokes of the wheel - to the rim."

"And then we'll be making our own electricity!" Nest boasted.

Dipped in the stream their grandfather had put to work, they were already generating a couple of kilowatts.

I was like one of those poor fish the poacher takes: shocked, paralized, gasping for breath. I should've let my eyes glaze over, there and then... float to the surface, give in.

"We're going to call her the Lady Luned," Menna said. "It was our great-aunt ... a bit of a madam, by all accounts."

"Though knowing us," said Nest, "that must be hard to believe."

She began to revolve in the flow, to turn over and over, a long white eel, laughing and feeling the cold sting on her shoulders and flanks (I could tell) forgetting that the rest of us were there, just savouring being alive and being Nest.

"Come on Glen, " Menna said, "let's go and get dry."

It got me fit, that climb... and back into The Brewer's Arms

Five-a-Side squad, though that might have had something to do with Jonno breaking his leg. All the summer and into autumn I was back and forward - up and down, really - while we worked on clearing the pond and refitting the sluice gate.

Sometimes they'd cook and we'd eat and bathe, bathe and eat behind the house, watching the wheel, knowing some day it'd turn again.

One weekend we painted the turbine shed bright green. Afterwards they lay in the low sun and traced strange patterns of tendrils and flowers and leaves on each other's hands and feet. Really tiny patterns, just with the point of a twig, like tattoos and clever, in a stupid sort of way.

"Poison that could be."

"Non-toxic paint," Menna smirked.

"You're mental," I said. "That's not gonna wash off, that isn't."

"It'll wear off, then," Chloe said. "Nothing lasts."

I'd spend the night - if I got the invite. I know what you're thinking.

Only one at a time.

Which one?

Well that was for them to know and me to find out and if you think that left me at a disadvantage, you've been caught once too often under a falling brick and not wearing your hard-hat.

November: from the tops, more often than not, Melin-y-ferched would be lurking in the smoke of its own chimneys and the mists of its own stream. In the shadow of Creigiau Llwyd, where the air never thawed, slate spoil lay underfoot like dirty slices of white bread. It was cruelly sharp stuff, each round jutting out for your ankles and shin-bones - or your hands if you lost it.

"Too dangerous, that walk home," Menna would say just at the last minute...the cow.

Oh, noticed the sudden drop in temperature did you?

Happened around about the time I got Conwy Man to deliver the new arm. You don't want to know what it took getting the bastard thing in place...so then there was the flaunch I'd promised. In the end they only needed the one.

Like I said, think ace of clubs: three perfect curves of metal into which the single arm slots, snug and neat, the last piece. I brought it up early Saturday morning and finished as the dusk fell.

Pale as milk, all of them, now the sun was long gone, three pasty faces watching as I threw the last of my stuff into the Jeep.

"Night-night, Glen," Menna said. I could hear the crackle of the kitchen fire, without glimpsing the flames imagine the red glow of its favoured circle.

Two, or rather four, could play at that game, I thought.

"Yeah, I've had it," I said. "I'll just clean up and I gotta be off."

"But you came in this," Chloe ran her fingers along the bonnet. Always playing the piano, she was, on one thing or another. "No one gets in if they come by motor."

"No exceptions," Nest said, gentle as ever. She stood in the doorway - barred the doorway - with the lamplight caressing her legs from thigh to instep and her long white skirt blown tight, streaming out behind like a dragonfly's wings.

I would've driven off then ... it's one of the few things a bloke can do with style. I would've if the Jeep had started, if the battery had had enough power left in it to light a chicken's fart.

A shortish walk, remember? I got home in time for breakfast, me and my broken knees and my chopped liver hands. Me and my busted ribs.

They mended.

It's spring again now. Menna and Chloe and Nest, they've started work on the turbine, I hear.

And big Mike, used to play in goal for The Brewers', works for Powergen .... saw him walking up the hill, the other day.

Someplace on the Veldt

Today he wasn't crying when he walked in but he had been: the thick blond lashes were still wet and his eyes were bloodshot as though it'd been swimming-pool afternoon which it hadn't. Like an arresting officer Jeff glanced at the boy's hands. They were scratched. Dirt was ground into the palms. Sometime during the last few hours he'd been down and Jeff could see it - the little body pitching forward, the thin skin raking the tarmac, trying to break the fall.

"Hello, Tom. How's it goin'?"

Jeff was trying for cheerful - difficult to pull off with a lump in the throat the size of a tangerine. But anything softer, anything nearer to what he really felt and he knew the boy would break down.

"Okay"

"You been doin' science today? Science first thing Wednesday isn't it?"

"Spellin' first, then Science."

"Get 'em all right?"

Tom shook his head but the movement lost itself in the more general heaves and tremors that started somewhere deep under the ribs and burst out through his mouth in a series of horrible rasps. His face turned from pale to crimson instantly, the way a blush flicks through a cuttlefish at the aquarium and then the boy was gone out of the room.

Jeff heard the stumpy legs, which he knew so well he could've modelled them in clay, pounding the stairs.

Overhead, Tom's bed creaked.

He walked into the kitchen to find Mandy. "What was it this time? What's the little bleeder done to him now?"

"Pushed him around." She didn't even look up from the raw chips she was dropping a handful at a time into the boiling oil. With each movement her fingers just skimmed the surface. It was as though she were offering them up to be scorched. "He took the money I gave him for breaktime, I think."

"You think?"

"Well I couldn't get Tom to tell me!" The potatoes had been too wet; the pan hissed and spat. Steam boiled up around her and laid a gauze on the window glass, cutting them off from the road outside, from the speeding traffic and evening dog-walkers out on the estate. "Understand Jeff - he doesn't always want to tell you everything. He has his pride. Sometimes it's best to talk and get it out, other times it's quiet he wants. You have to let Tom decide."

"That's crap! That's just bollocks, that is." He was angry at someone else, someone not present in the room. He was so angry that his fists kept bunching ready for that first satisfying punch and his centre of gravity shifted involuntarily back and forward so he could swing the whole of his cruiser-weight frame behind it.

"Don't get at me," Mandy said.

"I'm not." The humid kitchen spun. Spots of light popped into existence before his eyes. This was a thing that had never happened in the ring. It never happened in the job out there amongst the losers and wasters of half a dozen ugly little towns and a tatty length of coast. Nothing ever got to Jeff, everybody knew that.

He shook his head, trying to dislodge the shooting stars. "I'll go up. I'll go and see- "

"Leave it Jeff. I'll call him down in a minute. Let's just have our tea together. It's the first time you've been in this week. Just leave it."

"I can't leave it," he said but he sat at the table and concentrated on opening his hands. "If it was a grown-up I'd kill the bastard."

"That's a lot of good."

"You don't think that I would? 'Course I would. I'd do it and not give a toss what came after ... so long as Tom was all right."

If she had anything to say she didn't say it and he knew that was because he was starting to look bad...bragging, almost when he should be finding some way out for all three of them. Taking control - except that he couldn't control his own mouth. Off it went: " You know, I heard this bit on the radio the other morning - about a woman who had lived in Africa with her little girl - well all her family - but she's got this little girl, right? And one day they go out on safari - someplace on the veldt ... and they're goin' along in this landrover to see the animals and they, er, they get caught short. So the husband says to the guide to take them over to this patch of scrub 'cos it's all grassland, see? Just this one little bit of cover. And in they go, the woman and her little girl, and she's just got her knickers down when they hear this roar. There's a lion in these bushes with them! And the woman - and this is meant to be funny, right? - the woman runs for it. Just runs for it! There she is tryin' to get back in the van and hitch her knickers up all at the same time. Big joke, eh? Forgets her own child. Instinct, they said... like when you're drownin' and you pull the poor sap whose tryin' to save you under. Your body takes over, they said - nothin' you can do about it. But you know what I thought? You know what I kept thinkin' all day? Bitch, I thought - you bitch. That lion should've got you. Torn you apart. That's what you wanted... her own kid ... her own kid, for Chrissake!... I can't leave it."

Mandy stared at him as though he were speaking Welsh, which neither of them could.

She was right about Tom, though: nothing could stir the boy in his misery. He sat, listless, across from Jeff spearing each individual morsel on his fork, dipping it in the scarlet sauce and placing it back on the plate, hardly tasted.

"There's children in Africa would be glad of this," Mandy chided, Africa in her thoughts.

"They can 'ave it," said Tom.

"Shall we put it in a box? Mm? Put stamps on? See if the postman'll take it?"

He wouldn't look up.

"It'd make a big, greasy parcel! Go on then, if you're missing your programme. Your Dad'll bring you a choc-ice when we have our sweet."

Chin on chest, he slithered off.

In his head Jeff was rehearsing a dialogue, the way he did the night before court.

"Hello, Mrs Morgan-Tate. It's Jeff Humphries here, Tom's dad. Sorry to bother you at home ... you know how it is, working shifts, I can't always get into school and there was just something... I mean you don't want to make too much of it ... boys can be tough on each other... part of growing up... but this last year... longer maybe ... it's been more than just rough and tumble. Tom's very ... all the time ... a changed lad... just the one boy the real problem ... Yes, I do know ... Luke Warner..."

As the evening wore on the elements changed: "Sorry... this time of night ... quite important ... very worried ... you should be aware ... what Tom's going through...not just play... frightened ... bruises...Luke Warner... out of control..."

"I'm goin' to ring that headmistress."

"Don't," said Mandy.

"Jesus wept, woman, what's the matter with you?"

"I've seen the teacher. She's doin' her best."

"What?"

"Goin' to the head behind her back isn't helpin' Tom. You know what these people are like."

"They're paid to do a job, same as me - and they should bloody do it. Christ! The ... the shit I get into if some stinkin' drunk so much as breaks a fingernail bein' put in the van."

"Don't! You're not at work now... and anyway that part's of it - the job - him bein' a policeman's son. Can't change that ... and this is Saltney not Surrey. Tom's been called Pigspawn since the age of five. Pigspawn!"

She spat it. The pig was for him, it said, and Tom was the pawn. "Does well copin' with it too. He's had to - and it's not going to be any easier in the big school. But he's still got friends an' it's not as if it's all the time ... an' let's face it, what's Mrs Morgan-Tate goin' to do? They smashed the mirrors on her car last week."

"We've got to do somethin'." He knew it was the kitchen all over again with him needing a mark - just one clear mark - to place the punch. "Don't you care? Look at the state of him! He's nearly ten an' he's goin' about like a little old man!"

Tears rolled down her cheeks making him unreasonably furious.

If Tom could hold them back why couldn't she?

"Anyway, I can't stand by and do nothin' - even if you can."

"Oh, yeah? Well, send him to Eton - when you win the fuckin' lottery."

She was a lay-preacher's daughter and well over thirty and it was the first time she'd ever said it out loud.

In the distance he could hear the train ... and yet it must be miles away...the breeze, that would be it, the breeze in his face off the distant sea, wafting ahead of it a rhythmical clatter as the Holyhead express curved inward from the shore, tightening the breaks already for the Chester halt.

The boy heard it too. Jeff felt the muscles stiffen in his calves, so that he was forced to renew his grip on the scrawny ankles.

"Don't! Don't or I'll drop you! I'll just let go. Don't!"

Luke Warner dangled, limp. His smell was the sickly, shitty stench of the cells. He screamed. Jeff relaxed one hand.

"Shut it or you're gone now! This minute. One more sound and that's it."

It was dark beneath the bridge: a wide, black vacancy making the night sky look grey. That the track lay down there, bright and straight, he knew only from memory. Luke Warner knew it too ... and you had to give the boy credit: for a just-an-eleven year old, he was hard. 'A hard nut to crack' that's what Mrs Morgan-Tate had said - disappointing, really. You'd have expected something more original from a schoolteacher. But she was right, of course. Luke Warner was hard. He must have had to bite his own lips or tongue but he held on to it. He quietened.

"You could go under that train, boy. It'd squash you, easy - just like my boot when I step on a dog turd - nothing left, you know? Just the stink."

The boy's body was rigid again, as though it were not a living thing at all. Jeff thought he could've hoisted him back over the parapet and leaned him against it like a plank.

But he didn't haul him back ... he was about to ...he was just going to do it, just bracing himself for the slight effort when the lights in the distance caught his eye and they weren't red lights but they stopped him all the same ... stopped him and left him, clutching the bony, child's ankles... wondering what he was doing, wondering if he was really doing this, wondering if it would be all right and he could just - somehow - wake up and not be here.

Nom De Plume

And then the van door blew off overnight.

Neither Bomber nor Teg heard anything - nothing loud, nothing catastrophic, not even weird - but when they woke around eleven the rain was drifting down through the doorless doorway, stuff was lying all over the shop - well more stuff was lying all over the shop - and stuff was lying on them that hadn't been there when they'd passed out.

It was really quiet.

"Fuckin' 'ell," Teg said but this didn't alert Bomber to anything untoward because Teg said this every time he regained consciousness unless he was throwing up in which case he saved it till later.

"What?" said Bomber.

"We've bin burgled," said Teg.

"What?" said Bomber.

"Look at the fuckin' place, Bomber."

Bomber rested with his head against the window and groaned. He was leaving opening his eyes until he was up and about and started ramming into things...so that it would be more painful not to see than to see and then he would do it.

"Jesus," said Teg. Strange foam shapes lay across his chest. A midget's fire-extinguisher was cradled in his arms. "I mean, fuck. You've got to see this. Look at it will you? Some bastard's ripped the place apart."

Bomber looked. He found himself staring straight out to sea at a bright grey horizon. He couldn't understand what Teg was making all this fuss for. He screwed up his lids.

"Bomber," said Teg, "We're gonna have to move. Something's happened. I mean something big has happened. Bomber! Bomber don't go back to sleep, Bomber. Bomber! We're upsidedown."

Bomber moved his head and then took another squint through a strip of red eyeball. Teg was right. The caravan was upside-down and he and Teg and everthing else that could move inside it had moved and were lying all together in the curved hollow of its roof.

"What?" Bomber said, "I mean, what?"

He started to laugh. Teg started to laugh and they kept each other going. "I mean, what is this? We get turned over in the night an' we don't know?"

"That's it," said Teg.

"Well," said Bomber, "I tell you something, Teg. That's me an' your gran's diazepam finished. I told you it was bad shit."

"You didn't 'ave to take it. An' I told you not to mix it," said Teg.

"With what?"

"Everythin'," said Teg. "We mixed it with every fuckin' thing we had and this is the result."

"What, turning the van over? We never did this."

"No, not turnin' the van over. Not noticin' the van was over. That's what I mean!"

"Right," and then, "Time to get up," Bomber said.

They emerged from their coverings of picnic cups and saucers, little, wet, handmade tapestry cushions and crushed Tennents Super cans. Bomber was disgusted to find the empty plastic White Lightning bottles.

"What's the matter," asked Teg, "don't they sell cider in the Uni bar? "

"Not to me," said Bomber.

"Oh, right, Jeremy Bastard Bomber Paxman an' your starter for ten: Name the ten controlled substances that should not be mixed with White Lightning if you want to know when your caravan's gettin' rolled."

"Don't ever take to stand-up," Bomber said. "Cardboard City, that'll be you."

It wasn't easy to make sense of what had gone on outside; next to Teg's Gran's caravan which they'd just hauled themselves out of there was another van leaning up against it, and beyond that another and another like a row of big metal bales left in a field to dry. All the other vans that should've been in a semicircle around them were heaped up at the far end of the site, smashed and buckled, their contents spilled along the line of their destruction. The little thorn copse that had sheltered the vans was either under them or had been blown right out towards Caernarfon.

"Bog's gone," said Teg pointing to a heap of planks. "Gran'll go fuckin' spare."

"Loved that old crapper, did she?"

"I mean over everythin'. All this. She loved comin' 'ere."

"Ah-h."

"Fuck off."

"I'd do that if I could."

Teg looked at the wrecked vans. "Someone'll come, I bet. It'll be on the news." In the distance a bright red helicopter buzzed over The Lleyn. There was no wind and the still air was saturated - so wet it smudged the tops of the hills. "We must've been the only ones 'ere."

"In January. Yeah ... hey, Teg, praps we died, eh? We're really lying in the van, crushed and mangled, blood dripping into all those scatter cushions ... and those fuckin' glass dogs splintered in our faces ... this afternoon, your Dad and your Gran'll be up here weeping and wailing and we'll be dancing around shouting 'No, it's all right! We're here. We're saved. Just get us the fuck home!' But they won't hear us. They won't see us!"

"Can't see Dad an' Gran weepin' over you. They don't like you much."

"What? How can this be? Don't like me?"

"Think you're a junkie. They think you're all junkies at college - specially Liverpool."

"They're right – we are."

Teg didn't notice that Bomber was nettled.

"They say–"

"Yeah," said Bomber, "all junkies. Like Granny Diazepam."

"You didn't 'ave to take it. I just found it. I thought you'd wan–"

"Junkies, they all come on walking holidays in fuckin' January, don't they?"

"I'm off down the beach," said Teg.

Something had happened down on the beach as well. The white edge between waves and sand - because although it had calmed down this was still the Irish Sea having a go at dry Wales - the white edge or rather where the white edge should have been, was all fouled up with grey and clumps of black. It seemed as though some sort of hopeless, unevolved creatures were trying to make their first ever landfall but lacked the legs for it.

"Oil," said Teg. Teg's nose was pointed and thin as his face and his face was like a whippet's. "I can smell the fucker from here."

They scrambled over the lubricated shingle to the tide-line and Teg spotted the first bird huddled in the driftwood and old fish boxes. It appeared to be asleep. "Christ," said Bomber, "it looks how I feel."

The bird opened its eyes and shuffled to one side and yawned with a wide red gape. Its call - which anyone seeing how rough it looked would've expected to be hoarse - was a clear, high "Vee-bee! Vee-bee!"

"What the fuck is that?" Teg asked.

"How should I know? Eh? I don't know. The Lesser Backed Castrol Bird - how about that, eh? Or the ... the Four-Star Unleaded Flycatcher. Christ, who cares? What d'you think I'm doing at college - bird science or somethin'?"

They walked away, kicking at the oiled objects tossed up or finding clean pebbles and lobbing them into the oily slop. But even though they thought they'd chosen each missile with care there was black on their hands before long, black on their tan-cotton thighs.

"Hey," said Teg, "d'you reckon a ship's gone down? Praps there'll be bodies washed up ... or ... you know, cargo - stuff. Salvage - somethin' worth 'avin'."

"Toxic waste, the way things are going," Bomber said.

Every couple of minutes or so another bird writhed in the surf - so you couldn't tell if it was still trying to cling to existence or if it'd given up, was as unfeeling as the shingle, and the sea was making a mockery of anything that small and fragile ever having been alive at all.

"So," said Bomber, "how long before Granny Smackhead arrives to get us away?"

"Dad'll drive. Three hours from Wrexham, tops."

"Three hours from when they start out you mean."

"They'll come. I mean a storm or somethin' must've done all this, right?" What Bomber had to do was nod and he wouldn't even do that, making Teg feel like the bad-guy when all he'd done was offer Bomber a free week's holiday and free transport there and back and free tins courtesy of his Dad who was in work and free downers courtesy of his Gran only she didn't know it yet.

"They'll 'ave seen it on the telly. They'll come," said Teg hardly able to believe he was defending his Dad and Gran to Bomber, Bomber who'd been his best mate for seventeen years. "We could go back to the van ... find somethin' to eat."

Bomber kept walking.

"We could build a fire."

"Yeah," said Bomber. "Praps that helicopter'll take us outta this shitty place ... Christ what am I doing here?"

Bomber was staring out to sea as he shouted. Something moved at his feet.

"Don't tread on the poor little bleeder!" Teg said. The bird, a different, smaller model to the Vee-bee bird, hopped aside. "We could start collecting them... for when the bird-rescue people come."

"What?

Teg saw Bomber's face crack.

"Just get them together," he said. "What's so fuckin' funny about that? That's what you do when there's oil. Get 'em out, wash 'em and then put 'em back. That's what you do."

"Oh, that's what you do is it? Bird rescue? I spose there's nothing else is there?"

"What?"

"Well on the dole, that's what you spend your time doing? Gone green now, is it, Teg? Livin' up trees and bird rescue." Bomber picked up the corpse of a mud-coloured gannet and flapped its wings in Teg's face while the heavy head lolled back and then forward. "Bir-rd res-cue-e!"

The beak was a lance that nicked the skin along his cheek.

"Fuck off," he said.

"Y'know Teg, I think I'd rather be one of them junkie students your Dad's been telling you about."

"Fuck off."

"Bir-rd res-cue-e! Is it a bird? Is it a plane? No it's International Bird Rescue!"

Teg didn't have any choice now. He walked off and retrieved a Vee-bee bird that was dragging itself ashore, carried it tenderly up the beach and placed it in a hollow in the rocks. Then he went back, searching away from Bomber until he found a second. Bomber watched him try for a pair of gulls but they flew keening back to sea before he even got close.

Bomber went after him. "Don't be a dickhead! They just die. Whatever you do, they just die." Teg ignored him and Bomber had to walk with him or shut up. "Teg, man, you may as well wring their necks ... put them out of their misery." The squirming, doomed thing in Teg's hands roused itself a final time at the raised voices. It tore at Teg, drawing blood but he didn't even swear, laying it with exaggerated precaution next to another, walking quickly off again, not seeing it keel over. Bomber cursed and he wasn't cut. Teg continued until they must've gone a mile or more and now, when they could really have done with another casualty to diffuse the tension, there were no more birds.

"I'm going back," said Bomber, "Think I'll go back to the van - see if I can find where your Gran has her stash."

Teg turned with him or even before him - or it seemed that he did until Bomber felt the blow under his ribs and had no breath to call Teg all the things he wanted to call him. And still had no breath when he wanted to knock Teg onto the sand and start kicking his head.

By the time he caught Teg up he could see the old red Vauxhall parked above the beach and Teg's Dad was almost within shouting distance.

"What a storm, eh?" Teg's Dad shouted next second. "What a night. You all right?"

"I am," said Teg, "Bomber's a bit sore-"

"What a storm, eh?" Teg's Dad shouted again.

They clambered up to the car, Bomber wheezing.

Below them were left the little bird groups Teg had made, huddling together, all with their black and brown feathers, their black bills, sharp or hooked. They shuffled on the same shiny black feet - so that maybe even they didn't know what species they were anymore.

"Your Gran's really cut up about the caravan. Isn't that right, Mum? I was just tellin' the lads, you're really cut up about the van."

"Only metal," said Teg's Gran who had put on full make-up

for the mercy mission and some pearl beads and earings and the scarf Teg was meant to have bought her for Christmas. Her perfume outdid the oil. "Metal and things. Bugger me, it's a mess, though, isn't it? You boys all right?"

"I am," said Teg, "Bomber's a bit-"

"That's all right then. Where's there's no sense, there's no feelin', eh? We'll come over at the weekend and sort it ... too bloody depressing now. Got any stuff you want to take back?"

Bomber and Teg made towards the caravan which was shocking all over again in its dilapidation. "I phoned your Mam, Bomber," Gran called. "We're going to pick up Bomber, I said. He an' Teg must be all right or we'd've 'eard by now. D'you know what said? Who? she said." Gran cackled. "I'm going to pick up Bomber, I said. Who? she said."

Bomber turned. "I've haven't been Bomber for years. That's why. Nobody calls me Bomber anymore. It's Bruce now.'

"And why aren't I shocked?" said Teg.

Plasticity

"How are you managing, Simon?"
I don't know, Mrs Clare.
How am I managing?

It's got two meanings hasn't it? It could mean: how am I getting on? Or it might mean, how in Christ's name are you keeping going?

Well... this morning I stole some red and red-and-yellow patterned plastic mugs, three plastic spoons and a shiny, waterproof hat in that dark, posh-person's-wellies green. Also some more matches and a non-refillable lighter. All the kitchen cupboards are full of party plates and cups and I shouldn't really be storing them with sources of ignition ... or at least that's what people always say although it's not as if the matches are going to strike themselves, is it? Or the lighter's going to decide to pop up and present a flame to the multi-coloured serviettes in the middle of the night? Anyway, I thought better not take a chance, so all the paper goods will be going under the stairs from now on and if I get time I'll clear out the kitchen - the way things are going I'll be needing the space - and liberate some shelves in there.

It was a bit shitty, this morning, if I'm honest Mrs Clare. Apart from my other stuff I nearly got out with two white, glazed, disposable tablecloths edged with a design of holly leaves for some reason. I had my back blocking off the camera and neither of the girls could have cared less if I'd nicked the carpet tiles and the shop blinds, but would you believe it, some nosy old cow decides to keep me under observation? A stack of Rupert the Bear bowls in her hand, all ready to pay and yet every move I make, there she is. I mean, Jesus, you'd've thought she had shares in the store. Sixty if she was a day, probably got half a dozen grandchildren - giving them a treat... Spoilt little bastards, all of them, I'll bet.

That put me in a filthy mood and then there was this letter in the lunch-time post, signed by somebody called Tal Richardson, Head of Personnel. I'd never even heard of him. Talfryn, Taliesin? I'd've remembered a name like that - shows how long I've been off... not that I needed any pointers. Good old Tal had written to inform me I'd been 'on statutory sick leave for six months... and that in accordance with the terms of my contract the period of full pay had now expired.' Although, at the University's discretion, half my current salary might be payable for a further six months, it had been decided that in this case such payments would be 'inappropriate.'

It wasn't the money. What good is money to me, now? It must've been going into the account all this time but I'm buggered if I'd noticed. Lou had taken care of all of that, with her being in banking: money in, direct debits out - her system, just rolling on and on month after month, paying my bills. When I switched on the light Lou had arranged it, when I turned on the tap, that was down to her...

I dreamt about her last night. I think I dream about her every night but this one came back as I was walking home, crossing the river, with the plastic mugs and spoons bulging out my pockets. It started to rain but I left the water-proof hat where it was, tucked into my belt.

In the dream I was running along a towpath very close to the edge so that now and then I teetered on the old stones and nearly joined the rubbish floating in the canal - and that would've been really bad news because it was busy! Boats everywhere and of every type - brightly painted and pulled by horses, rusty old hulks chugging along on black smoke, sleek new cabin cruisers, the sort you see moored at Conwy and they wove in and out each other, never quite making contact but all the time I was thinking: this can't go on - someone's got to give way before there's one almighty fuck-up... and though I ran harder than ever, behind me I could hear that long, low note of metal scraping metal and splashing and screams as people were pitched in... and then I was out of it, that bit of the dream, anyway. The canal turned into the river at one of those deep, quiet stretches miles before it gets to Chester... fields along either bank, cows grazing, alder and willows - that sort of thing. I thought I could stop running now and enjoy it, sit down, relax, get my breath. Big mistake. The instant I looked into the water, there she was... there was Lou, lying just beneath the surface, her eyes closed, her long hair flowing away with the current, wearing the yellow trousers I'd sent to Oxfam but nothing else... the fish nibbling her arms ...nibbling at her breasts.

I turned aside when the dream came back to me - dived into Khan's newsagents and bought a paper and stole a see-through wallet full of coloured pens.

They'd found a woman's body on the beach at Prestatyn... a very old woman - wandered away from a home. Another old woman... they were getting to be the day's talisman... a very old woman only missing one night.

Thank God it was a bloke that came later on to buy the dining room stuff.

"Dr Phillips isn't it?"

It's a small town ; three, four months later I'm still its media star.

"Yeah, come in."

I'd expected some seedy little operator with an ancient truck, instead here was Mr Three-Piece-Suit clutching his BMW keys.

"We've been looking for old mahogany for ages ... I think anything the dealers get round here goes straight to the shippers ... off to America, or at least that's what I've been told."

"Uh-huh.

If he noticed the dust he didn't comment. "Oh, that's nice ... um. Yes, quite plain but nice." He ran his hands down the tapering table legs as though examining a horse ... what did he expect? That the ball-and-claw foot would flick backwards as it did for the farrier, falling into the palm ready to be shod?

"Any..um...restoration?"

"My wife's father re-upholstered the chairs. That was his trade before he retired."

Stupid, stupid. That was still his trade. Time hadn't taken his skill, his patience, his dexterity away.

"Yes, I'm sorry."

What for?

"They're very ... very well-done. Six hundred?"

I nodded. The pale eyes flicked around the room, although it was completely bare save the objects under discussion. Perhaps he made his living selling things, cars or kitchens or swimming pools and these natural instincts were at war with his bienseance.

My status – my victim status – must've given me the edge. He gave a huge sigh that set the dust swirling between us. "Fine, fine. Half now and the rest when they're picked up? I'll get one of the lads to call round with the van."

He counted out fifties onto his table. At the door he said, "I'm sorry... but, well, there's no news is there, about your wife?"

"No news."

"I'm sorry."

"Yes, thank-you."

I've never met anyone who wasn't.

When he'd gone I ate some sandwiches off a pink paper plate from a new pack I'd just started... in the dining room that is three metres wide and four long and two-and-a-half-high... that has existed in this shape for one hundred and sixteen years. I know this because the plasterer had signed his work and it was still there, waiting, when we stripped the room: John James, 1875.

A lovely old room, Lou called it... her favourite with its flowers and leaves twining along the cornices and its wainscotting and its polished floor. Hardly old, I'd told her. The universe was created over twenty billion years ago.

And she'd laughed. Means nothing, she'd laughed. Twenty billion means nothing like in money. Twenty-billion years, twenty billion pounds – what's that to us, she'd said.

Did you know that when the universe began there were twenty-six dimensions?

Up, down, across, age... and the others? Curled up very small, too small for us to perceive. Still there. In our three by four by two-and-a-half dining room, still there after one hundred and sixteen years.

Everything that's ever existed is still there.

Somewhere.

Like Lou.

When whatever-his-name-is picks up his stuff - he did tell me his name but its gone - that'll be it. Sofas, beds, tables, chairs, pictures, cupboards and every other bit of paraphernalia ... all gone. There are people advertising in the paper that'll do the lot. House clearance, they call it ... but I needed it to go piece by piece just as we'd bought it.

There is just one other thing: the car. Yesterday morning the phone rang and it was the North Wales police, not all of them, you understand, just a Sergeant Toms, anxious to make it clear he was calling for Inspector Vaughan. Inspector Vaughan was meant to be finding Lou. It seems I could have my car back.

"But what about the evidence?" I said. "There was a bloodstain on the steering wheel and a sort of scratch or scuff on the front seat - a new one...and cellophane from a pack of cigarettes though neither of us-"

"That's all done with," he said. "It's photographed, sampled and documented. If anything ever came to court all the forensic is there."

If anything ever...

"...and the stuff in the tyres that told you it had been on a beach where there was also mud. And that grey substance, like melted plastic-"

"Yes, sir," he said. "All the evidence - it's been gathered. Really, we can't get much else. It was your only vehicle, as I remember. You may as well have it back."

"I don't want it back. I want you to keep it and find my wife."

"I'm sorry, sir," was all he said.

That grey substance ... I bet they still don't know what it is. It was grey ... and there were drops of it, hardened drops ... three big drops. "Give me a sample," I'd said. "Let me take it in to the Faculty. I'll get them working on it if you can't find out." Oh, no. Not one minute sample - and now they're offering a whole sodding Ford Escort back.

The more I pleaded to get the grey plasticy substance looked at - like melted plastic it was, not paint - the more I offered, the less they seemed to care.

"I'm a scientist," I said, "let me-"

"Not a chemist though – not a plastics man, eh?"

They never believed I didn't know about the grey substance - about Lou.

They think I'm a storyteller.

I'm useless at making things up. But I would like to try. I'd like to invent a story about what's been happening to Lou all this time. Right from the afternoon our car went north and parked on a beach for a time that wasn't a proper beach because there was sand and mud that might have been out of a river in the tread.

If it was a good enough story it could do a variety of things: one, it could describe how she's been living without any of those civilized supports we panic when we lose, like money and keys and documents saying who we are. And stupid but really important things - calendula cream for the eczema on her elbows, a little blue box, like a pen-case, for tampons... that novel with only a few pages to finish and due back at the library within the week ...and shoes.

All her shoes were still in the bottom of the wardrobe before I sold it. She had six pairs and some red leather trainers and some soft mocassins we bought in Canada she used as house shoes. They were all there: a double row of four.

Why was she not wearing the mocassins if she was taken away from inside? And why, when I mentioned the eczema did Vaughan stop writing and look me straight in the eye (as per training, I guess) and say, "Eczema? Your wife suffered from eczema - did it bother her much... or you? Did you still find her attractive?"

Whoever took her - or she went with - wanted her barefoot?

He thinks I killed her over eczema?

Oh, aye, that'll be right.

I heard Robbie Coltrane say that on T.V. - a great summation of the impossible, yeah? Though you needed to hear him do it.

Two - this story could explain how she's been doing without me - sounds egotistical, I know, a male thing, but it's not. For ten years Lou and I lived so close you couldn't have slipped a card, say the ace of spades, between us. What I knew, she knew. We never had a night apart. I've sold the bed and I never slept once in it without her... not just without her, without touching her. Neither of us knew what it was to be physically alone.

I can never decide on the number of characters when I write it – this story...this story I write at night. I know there'd be me and Lou and at least another. At least another.

Three: this wonderful fable would have an ending, a twist that had her walking back into the house with words that would bend Time and snap it all back the way it was.

How am I doing, Mrs Clare? Well, I'm doing all right.

I've stopped hearing 'Missing bank clerk' at the start of the news.

I've had the garden dug over twice, for free.

Today I sold the dining room furniture and I've got my eye on a white moulded set on a patio in Telford Avenue. Five pieces - I'll take it overnight. And that'll be the house finished. Full of nice bright disposable ware, ready for that moment Time bends and snaps back and Lou walks in on her bare feet.

Every dimension bends. Time? You can go back along it.

'With one bend we were free'.

It's a misquote. Lou knows of what.

Balance

As Del was getting dressed she said, "He's away all next week... conference on the under-achieving child .... Llandudno or Colwyn Bay or some other dead an' alive hole."

The tie knot wasn't working. He wrenched it apart and began again. "Oh, right."

"Well don't sound so bloody ecstatic about it!"

"No ... I mean, that's great."

"Don't go doing me any favours."

Wendy's already thin lips had contracted to a single line. If Del didn't think quickly the afternoon would end in a spitting match and a sulky goodbye. This would be unjust when you considered how much credit he should have clocked up for a performance that had finished not ten minutes ago.

"Look love," he said still not having an idea in his head as to how to continue. In the mirrored wardrobe, he caught sight of his own short, dark hair - short enough not to need combing but not so short as to frighten the clients. Would it be okay to be fastening on his watch as he talked? Better not - might seem that he was desperate to get going, which he was. "Look, it's not that... that I'm saying I'm not glad he's away..." Her eyes lost none of their hostility but that was probably more to do with the double negative than his hitting the wrong note. He ploughed on. "But I s'pose I just don't like to be reminded of the fact that I only get you when it suits him."

She laughed. "Oh-h! Jealous puss."

Bit by bit he released the great lungful of breath put away instinctively by a subconscious predicting fight or flight. So easy to go into the red, Delwyn, he told himself. A moment's inattention and there were the future profits for the next half-year wiped straight off your books.

In one casual movement he managed to slump down onto the bed to face her and slip both feet into his shoes. The Rolex - now just millimetres from his left hand - showed quarter to three. If he could be out in anything less than eight minutes then even with the worst the Chester traffic had to throw at him Benson's Garage was a still distinct possibility by four.

Two billable hours, that's what he needed. It all depended on the next response.

"Why don't I get us a drink?" he offered loading his voice with quiet depression.

Wendy turned onto her back so that a pair of large, snowy breasts popped out to perch on the rose-coloured quilt. Despite their size they were held steady and in place by really excellent pectorals. "Not poss, I'm afraid. Got to pick up the girls. Can't have the head's wife at the school gate with a satisfied smile on her face and reeking of booze."

He invested a few seconds in an intense stare.

"Right. Fine. I'll take my unreasonably jealous self off then."

He palmed his watch and signet ring, planting a kiss on the end of her nose.

Six-ten saw him slaloming the green TVR out through the MOT failures that old Benson kept around for his boys to cannibalize. He had failed to talk his literally oily client out of an expansion scheme that was bound to bankrupt him... still there was a nice little earner preparing the doomed business plan - and the promise of some nearly free clutch-work when he dropped it off.

"That clutch needs some-"

"I know," Del countered as he joined Chris in the car-park of The Greyhound. Chris lusted after the little motor so was keen to nitpick. "I know - noticed it this morning. Eight o'clock I thought, Delwyn, that's a two-fifty sort of noise if ever I heard one and by close of play it was booked in at Benson's for one-two-five off the bill...he'll do it end of the week."

"Are we still ... ?" Chris was his partner but he liked to pretend ignorance of the seedier side of the market, even though it provided most of their income.

"Course we are. Come on." Del hurried him through the door with a slap on the shoulder that wasn't all that light or playful. "The usual, Mags!"

To Chris he said, "I'm on a schedule. I've only got time for the one."

"What?"

Chris, the family man, just couldn't help asking. He knew it was going to sting, knew it was going to be a real downer to carry back to the wife and kids...but it was like picking a nice crusty scab. "I thought you'd been playing teachers and-"

"Pets. Yeah I have. Nice little golden guinea-pig, squeals a lot, loves a bit of exercise."

"Oh come on. She must be knocking on for forty."

"Ex-P.E. mistress. Makes all the difference."

Chris's eyes became dark slits in the shade of the bar. "Oh, God."

"Yeah, I know. Aren't I the lucky bugger?"

"Not that as well?"

"Haven't tried Wendy... and certainly not the lovely Catrin ... not yet, anyway."

Chris's expression turned from prurience to panic. "Catrin Benson?"

"Thought you could hardly remember who Benson was," Del snapped. He knocked back his colourless drink and caught the landlady's attention. "N'other one of them, Mags. Same again?"

Chris had hardly touched the lager and shook his head. "I remember Catrin. Benson used to think the sun shone out of that girl's-"

"Still does...and it is a particularly fine example. I could almost believe it myself."

"For Chris sake what are you messing around there for? She's just a kid."

"Eighteen. I got the catering for the birthday bash put through as business entertaining. Works for her dad but thinks - get this -" he slipped into a sing-song accent, "- she might like to go into accountancy. You can guess what I nearly said to that ... boyfriend's in Bosnia."

"So where do you fit in?"

"Oh the usual place. D'you need a route map?"

Even without the drink Chris was able to get instantly angry. The flush spread right the way up to his receding hairline and it kept on going through the scrubby, woodland-edge effect that covered his scalp. "You know what I'm on about! We've had this out before. I don't like you arseing about with clients."

"Don't talk shit. I'm not doing it to Benson in the back of his workshop - I'm taking the daughter out for a cheapish Chinese and a free shag."

Chris relaxed and stared into his flat half-pint. "Well watch it, eh? We don't want to lose the account."

"Trust me. Anyway, Benson'll be a patch of diesel on the forecourt by the end of next year."

"That bad?"

Del ran one finger across his throat.

"Oh well, you can't win 'em all."

Del was incensed. "Course you can! You defeatist old sod! Course you can win 'em all. Look at me! Take today." He whipped out a slim, black leather organizer which he consulted, clearly knowing what he would find.

"Just you take today. Eight-thirty till eleven, worked on the Jones Brothers audit, then an hour down the street at Jacksons - very convenient and a new redhead in reception - then twenty minutes with Mrs Graham - husband on a binge again and giving the manageress one, where does that leave her money? Answer: down the toilet - before swift departure to Mallard Cottage – views of the estuary, feathered things with the big feet, clouds, boats, realistic gas-log fire, that sort of stuff – and Wendy Willing ready to give me lunch and her all. Hey Mags!"

The elderly woman took her time about coming over, even though the bar was near-empty. "Mags, my sweet, how much would a slice of paté, mixed salad - interesting, you get it? - French bread, cheeses and a couple of glasses of, um, Cape Red set me back?"

"We just do sandwiches Monday nights."

"Yes, I know that. I'm not asking that. Much as I'd love to eat in your charming establishment I've gotta be off." Del glanced at his watch. "Soon. What I mean is how much would it cost on a night when you were doing it?"

"Paté and a roll," she intoned - Del spluttered but the woman remained straight-faced- "would be three-fifty, salad another two. Cheese? Well that'd have to be cheese and biscuits - that's two-eighty and two glasses of red - two fifty. That's-"

"Ten pounds eighty," Chris and Del said in perfect synch.

"Anything to drink?"

"No thanks," Del said. He turned to Chris. "So add to that an hour and a half's imaginative bonking in comfortable surroundings - well-sprung bed, en suite facilities, matching tissues, very clean - you've gotta be looking at a hundred - a hundred quid easy."

"I wouldn't know," said Chris.

"Me neither, that's the point. Never paid. Okay, where was I? Wendy's - so let's say I take the cost of the lunch off as nuisance money 'cos - and I'm being scrupulously honest here - she did get a bit naughty on the how-much-do-you-love-me-front. But I won't agree to any further debits from your basic hundred. Oh no. I got to Benson's for the full two hours, halved the cost of the clutch-job... and came away on a promise."

Del downed the second drink, seeming ready to move off. "So, tonight I'm looking at - what - forty quid at The Ming?"

Chris nodded.

"Back to my place ... maybe two brandies? What'll I charge her? It's good stuff but let's be generous ... let's say a quid apiece. It's not as if I'm licensed premises - don't want to get greedy. Then we have to be budgeting for an all-nighter. She's got tomorrow off for working a Saturday for her sweet old dad. Come on, now, what's your best guess at that? Even if we're talking something totally straight? What'll you do me for bed-and-breakfast with Catrin? Three hundred? Four? I mean, have you seen those legs?"

"A lot must depend on location," Chris suggested. "Huge difference in property prices between Chester, Wrexham, Mold or Flint. A tart's gotta have a home! But let's say you're staying in Wales for it... Mold... well, low turnover in Wales ... Mold ...let's think - not that much organized. Can't compare prices with somewhere like the West End - there the girls'll be stuck with fixed overheads - an agency or a pimp."

"There's that round here - and it's supply and demand. London you'd have more girls chasing finite business."

"No, no," Chris wasn't having any, "a well-run enterprise will create its own demand."

"Granted. I'll try that line on Wendy, with slight alterations, you know. But to stick to the point, even if you beat me down to three hundred on the Catrin transaction, I'm two-fifty-eight plus one, plus one-twenty-five on the car - that's four-hundred and eighty-three plus six-and-a-half billable hours ahead."

Del turned and swept up the keys to the TVR in one easy action. "Oh, that's minus four-pounds-eighty."

"What for?"

"You know what for, you tight sod. A round and a half of drinks ... again."

Mother Die

"Deb! Deb! Did you do number seven? Did you? Go on - tell us!"

Two youngish girls stood at a Hawarden bus-stop, narrow backs to the chill air straight off Moel Fammau's white top. They were chewing like a couple of ruminants. One held a lighted cigarette on which she puffed more often than any seasoned smoker would have done, yet still managed to inhale without upsetting the regular motion of her jaw. Sensibly she was leaving communication to her friend.

"Deb!"

The two were being approached by a third. "Deb!"

Deb arrived beside them without response to the summons.

"Are y'with us yet, eh? I said: Did you do number seven?"

Deb surveyed the on-coming traffic as it crawled past. The driver of a van - FLINTSHIRE FOODS! BIG BAPS FOR SMALL BUSINESSES!- tapped the windscreen, trying to gain her attention but Deb's eyes remained stubbornly unfocused. The two original keepers of the bus-stop sighed, exchanged glances, looked up to heaven and tutted.

"That was your Jean in that van," said one.

"Oh, don't talk to 'er, "said the other, "she's doin' it on purpose. She's mad, she is."

They pretended to occupy themselves with other things: poking around in sports bags at their feet or suddenly staring hard (as if in recognition) at complete strangers passing by.

"Deb!" said the smoker.

Deb's pale and pretty face remained blank and her manner abstracted but a very slight tightening of the muscles about her mouth soon spread downwards, skirting the dimpled chin and running on into her neck. Her eyes bulged - her cheeks flushed. All three girls, seemingly at the same instant, were engulfed by a wave of giggling. It swept across them - left them weak and mutually supportive. When the coach arrived, they were glad to get on.

Once aboard, the smoker detached herself to join a black girl at the back. Deb and friend settled themselves near the door.

"Deb."

"What?"

"Did you do number seven? It's the one about-"

"No, I didn't do number bloody seven! An' I didn't do numbers one to bloody six, neither. All right?"

"All right!"

There was no more talk for minutes after this. A distinct coolness between them, they moved from each other's touch on the seat.

"Julie."

"Mm?"

"Can I copy yours at break?"

" 'aven't done number seven."

"Well some of the others then?" Deb wheedled. "Just two or three of the others - just to look as if I've done somethin'."

"Yeah," said Julie, "but I dunno why you can't do 'em y'self. You're better than me. I bet you could get an A if you-"

"You wouldn't 'ave done 'em! Not if you'd sat with my gran all night. Me mum went out, didn't she? I 'ad to sit with 'er till 'alf past ten."

Julie remained unimpressed. "Well! I 'ave to look after our Rhys. It couldn't be worse than that. I'm never gonna 'ave kids! Honest - I couldn't take it. There's nothing worse than kids."

"There is. My gran." As Deb spoke she contorted her face and pursed her lips. Momentarily, she assumed a look of great age.

"Well at least your gran don't wet the bed," said Julie, not noticing.

"'ow do you know?"

"Well does she?"

"She might," said Deb.

"But does she?"

" Yeah - no-o ... but I 'ate her all the same."

"I do 'ate my gran," said Deb. She and Julie were back in their seats on the coach but travelling in the opposite direction.

"You don't."

"I bloody do. My mum 'ates 'er too – though she tries not to let on. We both 'ate 'er."

"Ah well," said Julie profoundly, "praps she'll die soon."

"I bet she won't."

"She'll 'ave to," reasoned Julie. "She's really old."

"'ow old do you think she is?"

"'undred," said Julie making them both laugh.

"She's sixty-bloody-nine," said Deb when they'd finished.

"Well that's old."

"Not old enough," said Deb, darkly.

Mrs Nelson lay beneath the quilt holding her breath. She was straining to catch the click of her grandaughter's key as it engaged the lock on the back door. She'd heard the gate swing to. The girl was on her way.

"Deborah! Is that you?" she called. A soft thud was the only reply that came drifting up. She knew that sound. That was the hall cupboard closing. So - the little madam had crept in, had she? And meant, probably, to creep out again as quickly.

"Deborah! I know you can 'ere me. You come on up!" The woman struggled forward in bed, the better to project her voice. "Now!"

Silence.

She must be sitting at the bottom of the stairs, Mrs Nelson decided.

"Deborah! I know you're in that 'all."

There were no footsteps but the banister gave a loud creak as though a huge weight had settled on it. The little devil was sitting on the flat bit where the stairs turned the corner.

"When your mother comes in I'll 'ave something to say to 'er."

The banister gave another creak.

"Deborah Nelson, get up them stairs!"

The bedroom door flew open to reveal the girl. A short red coat hung on her shoulders over a grey school uniform.

"Me name's not Nelson! It's Deborah Bowen!"

"Oh, goin' out are we, Little Red Riding 'ood? Well, you're to stay in - your mother's workin' late. Your mother said. Your mother - remember 'er? Sandra Nelson. Don't you go mentioning the name Bowen in this 'ouse again."

Next day Julie had a suggestion.

"You could frighten 'er to death."

"Are you kiddin'? My gran'd make Dracula faint. Frighten 'er? She looks like a werewolf."

Julie tittered. "Go on!"

"Yeah," said Deb, "she does. Honest. You 'aven't seen 'er for ages. She looks like a wolf - well a wolf that's 'ad all its teeth out."

"Merle! Merle!" Julie called, "Deb's gran looks like a wolf."

"Yeah?"

"Yeah - honest," said Deb.

The black girl moved on.

"You should get Merle to put a curse on 'er," said Julie. "I bet she could. She said her auntie could put curses on people."

"Don't be daft," said Deb. "She's a dinner lady."

The dinner that day - not served by Merle's auntie - was everything Deb didn't like - cheese and onion pie and baked beans, stewed apple and yoghurt. Deb sat and ate the beans one by one with her fork while the pudding congealed.

"You're the only person I know that doesn't like beans," Julie observed.

"My gran doesn't like beans."

"Your gran!"

"You know what I 'ate most about 'er? She smells. She just lies in that room all day – she won't get up - and it smells of her. You can smell it everywhere."

"Why doesn't she get up?"

"She 'ad a stroke, asn't she? All down 'er left side or somethin' - not the left side of 'er tongue though...or at least it got better quick enough. She can use that okay."

"Praps she'll die," said Julie.

"Praps."

"You seen Merle's ears?"

"Yeah," said Deb.

"I might 'ave mine done."

"Too cold," said Deb, "- you shouldn't 'ave them pierced when it's cold. They go bad."

"Yeah," said Julie, "I spose I could wait till it's warmer ... but I bet it's gone up by then."

Deb and Julie hardly noticed the seasons. In the shops were the spring's new skirts and tops that you needed a summer job to get ... and clothes and money were more important than what the weather was doing or what was growing where.

When the days lengthened they used it as an excuse to stay out even later. At the bus-stop they were red-eyed and still pale. One morning Deb found herself alone. She was instantly bored.

She tried leaning with her back against the bus shelter and stared into space - but this made her yawn and yawning gave you lines around your mouth. She'd have to walk up and down just to stay awake. She sauntered along in the direction the coach would come from where the bare road of the scruffy estate dwindled into a lane. Hawarden ended here – the country, such as it was, began... and there was a sort of biological seepage at work, the dog-turds, used condoms and old Chinese meals going one way, the slurry, the pink baler-twine and stench of the poultry death camps the other. The weeds were blooming in the untended cottage gardens with thistles and brambles poking through the dusty, unclipped evergreens... and at the bottom of one hedge, a crop of white flowers...

Deb pulled her hand away as if she'd been stung. She thought she knew what they were and didn't want to touch - oh, no thank-you!

On the coach she pretended not to see Merle and sat by herself.

"Lo," Merle said.

"Lo."

"Where's them two?" asked Merle, with a nod to the retreating bus-stop.

"Scivin' or sick, I spose," she answered but Shut your mouth, Merle, she thought, I'm trying to remember ...

There were daisies for chain-making and buttercups to see if you liked butter ... there were dandelions that made you pee yourself and told the time in seed ... and purple clover, sweet at the base of the petals ... there was four-leafed clover that you could never find and was lucky ... and dock to cure nettle stings ... and there was Mother Die.

Mother Die. If you took it into the house, it would kill your mother - probably straight away.

Julie turned up again next morning.

"Y'know that white stuff ... ?" said Deb.

Julie burst out laughing. "No!"

"You do! You know! That white stuff that grows everywhere. A flower."

Julie wrinkled her forehead but still looked ready to giggle. "Yeah."

"Do you?" Deb demanded.

"Yeah, I've said."

"Well... when you were little, did they tell you that if you took it into the 'ouse your mother would die?"

"Go on! Yeah! No! Not if you took it into the 'ouse... it was just if you picked it."

"It wasn't."

"It was!" said Julie.

"It was if you took it in."

Julie shook her head.

"That's daft," said Deb. "It was if you took it in!"

"No it wasn't. I remember-"

"Oh 'ow would you know?" asked Deb, exasperated. "You're friggin' thick, that's what you are."

Because Julie was sulking Deb went to the library on her own. She was not a frequent visitor to the place. Too embarrassed to ask for help she was forced to hunt around for most of the dinner hour. Finally she unearthed a dog-eared and dirty volume from which most of the prettier pictures had been torn. 'Wild Flowers of Britain' looked fit only for the compost heap.

There was no Mother Die. The weed seemed to have escaped the notice of the eminent naturalist who'd written the book. There were lots of plants with Latin names, though, and clusters of white flowers: Achillea millefolium, Daucus carota, Anthricus silvestris, Aegopodium podagraria - not to mention Heracleum sphondylium. None of them seemed to mean Mother Die and the book offered no guide to the fatal potential of each plant. Only Deadly Nightshade might fit that particular bill.

Deb was forced to accost a startled teacher and describe the object of her quest – though not its usage.

"It might be Sweet Cecily," he offered.

"Don't think so," said Deb.

"What you doin'?" someone asked.

Deb spun round to find Merle and Sue the smoker watching her. She had been poking about in the tall grass and nettles that

106

bordered the playing field. Immediately she straightened up and put her hands in her cardigan pockets.

"You lost somethin?"

"Yeah," said Deb.

"What you lost?"

"Me ring," said Deb easing the little cameo off her finger and letting it fall into the safety of the wool.

"Shall we 'elp you look?"

"Please," said Deb.

The two girls squatted down and began to part the shorter, new-mown grass, keeping well away from the nettles.

"Where's Julie?" Merle asked.

"'ow should I know?"

They continued to search but failing to find the ring in the first few minutes, lost heart. Soon they were sitting on the turf watching Deb as she doggedly hunted for the ring in her pocket.

"You an' Julie 'ad a row?" suggested Sue.

"Sort of."

"What about?"

"Oh, nothin'."

They considered this behind Deb's back, exchanging knowing looks.

"You could come round with us if you wanted," said Merle.

" 'ello Mum! "

"Deb! 'ello love. What you doin' 'ere?"

"Just come to meet you, didn't I?"

"Well that's nice." Deb's mother glanced at the canvas bag that served as a satchel. "Not been 'ome?"

Deb hesitated. "Yeah," she said.

"You should've left your bag - you drip!" She took her daughter's arm. "Is your gran all right?"

"Dunno."

"Didn't you look in on 'er?"

"Didn't go in, did I?"

"Oh, Deb!"

Deb grinned.

"What you been doing' at school, then?"

Deb had to think hard. "The... Slave Trade," she came up

with, and then to add a touch of authenticity, "makes you feel a bit.. you know... sittin' next to Merle."

This was inspired.

They were still in sight of the grand entrance to Hawarden Castle, ancestral home of the Gladstones. "If anyone should feel a bit you know, it's those buggers in there," Deb's mother said. "Took them long enough to feel you know, I'll bet."

Wearily they made their way through the village and out onto the estate." Tell you what," Deb said, "you take this bag an' I'll take your shoppin'. Looks as if it weighs a ton."

The shopping was as heavy as it appeared and they had to stop several times while Deb transferred it from one reddened hand to the other - but she refused to give it up. At one such stop her mother's eyes rested casually on her own burden ... and on the various bits of greenery planted amongst Deb's books.

"What 'ave you got in 'ere? There's all weeds and stuff."

"Botany," said Deb.

When they reached home, Mrs Nelson was shouting before they were through the door.

"I'll 'ave to go up for a minute," said her mother. She dropped Deb's bag just inside on the hall floor. Deb gave it a nudge with her toe so that it fell forward, scattering heads of hogweed, yarrow, wild carrot and cow parsley across the red tiles. She was taking no chances - had gathered everything that grew with the right sort of flower. Some, picked from the playing field that morning were already wilted while others grabbed from the bus-stop environs were pungently fresh.

She waited till the very last second before sweeping away her specimens. Her mother was on the bottom stair as Deb ran out to the bin, a spicy, herbal scent filling her nostrils and returning on her hands.

She just hoped the Mother Die – whichever it was - had had long enough to do its job.

Deb waited.

Nothing happened that evening and Mrs Nelson retired, apparently in no danger. The following morning she woke. Deb suffered deep disappointment. She began to have doubts ... perhaps the flowers needed to be kept in over night ... perhaps till they withered ... perhaps her mother had to want to kill Mrs Nelson or at least know about bringing the Mother Die home.

Perhaps, after all, she'd not found the right flower.

By Monday morning, Deb had stopped believing it would work. Why, after all, should it? Buttercups didn't tell if you really liked butter, did they? Four-leafed clovers probably weren't lucky and that was if you could find them... Julie's little brother wet the bed nightly without the aid of dandelions and Mother Die didn't get rid of a mother even when you brought it into the house.

Julie was at the bus-stop as usual. In the absence of Sue she was inclined to be friendly.

"Merle said you lost your ring."

"I found it," said Deb.

"Oh, good. It's nice, isn't it?"

"Yeah - me mum bought it."

"Your mum, she's really nice, isn't she?"

Deb didn't feel like talking to Julie. She was too depressed. She wanted to stand there and just watch the traffic go by - red car, white car, lorry, lorry, blue car, black car, police car ...

"'ow's your gran?" Julie asked with a confidential smirk. "Still alive, is she?"

"Worse luck."

"I asked about that Mother Die, you know. I was right - it's if you pick it your mother dies."

"It'll never get better if you pick it," said Deb dreamily.

Lorry, motor-bike, white car, black car, motor-bike, van, ambulance....

"It's if you pick it," Julie said, "not if you take it in the 'ouse. I knew I was right." Deb spun her around.

"Oh what would you know! You're fuckin' thick, that's what you are."

They travelled on separate seats from then on and somehow failed to see each other when they met. It wasn't until a month had gone by - and her mother failed to come home one night - Deb discovered Julie was right.